A
WORLD
FIT FOR
GRIMSBY

A
WORLD
FIT FOR
GRIMSBY

HILARY EVANS

ST MARTIN'S PRESS

NEW YORK

for Mary (naturally)
and for Richard Roud too (of course)

All you whose Vse is
To court the Muses
    In this barbarick Clime,
      Go to: you waste your Time.
Alas your suit
Will neuer boot,
    They neuer will abide
    In this cold Contriside.

NICOLAS GRIMSBY
Satyr Exhorting the Poets of Northumbria
to Abandon their Profession and Return to
their Sheep-Stealing.

'WHERE please do I find the vaysay?'
I pointed out as exactly as I could the where-
abouts of our Municipal Gents, a little way up the
High Street, sandwiched between Smiths and the Lady Jane
Tea Rooms. My inquirer thanked me in guttural tones and
precipitated himself into the bowling bustling traffic — a fat
dazzled man in rimless glasses and checkered knickerbockers,
flowered shirt and white stockings.

A Dutchman, I calculated, as I swung my leg over the
saddle of my bike and pedalled off down the street, avoiding
as best I could an American lady standing right out in the
roadway among the cars and buses to photograph the actual
outside of the very room where she had truly slept last
night. Now, in my second year in Riddleford, it had become second nature to allow for the eccentric behaviour
of our tourists: and I had become, too, quite an expert at
distinguishing the various species of foreign visitors who
come swarming up into Northumberland to see our sites
and sights. All last summer through I had seen them goggling in groups, shepherded with a smile by Fothergill Jones
the Official Guide — over The Birthplace (50 mins.), St.
Bridget's Parish Church (25 mins.), and Lady Jane's Cottage
(20 mins. if you skip the Helliwell Goose Memorial Exhibition of Victorian moustache-cups).

As I biked on through the Town Centre I could see that the Season was with us again this fine April morning. The first heralds of the invasion force were already to be seen.

My ancient black bike with its Come-To-Jesus handlebars was humiliatingly overtaken by the first bare-shinned cyclists from the Youth Hostel. Hearty youths with low-slung gaudily-tinted machines, all levers and knobs and plastic things to drink from, making no sound as they whizzed past except for an exciting whine of hardblown tyres on tarmac. The males wore short corduroy shorts and striped shirts with esoteric badges, admitting them to who knows what secret club-rooms in strange northern cities: their saddlebags were heavy with sleeping-bags, their pockets bulged with spare inner tubes. Their girls wore even shorter shorts and high-pitched busts thinly coated with skimpy Aertex — a sight to give you ideas of joining a club yourself and taking up cycling seriously till your eyes light on their calves.

The massive automobiles of the first Americans were parked outside the most half-timbered of our hotels. Outside them on the sidewalks pattered the first Americans themselves, their shoulders bowed beneath the crippling weight of cameras and meters and sling-bags and glasses.

Pedalling across the Market Square, I saw one of this year's first chara-loads of British matronhood emerging from their coach — saw them shake themselves, smooth their flowered dresses, clutch their shopping bags, and look about with aggressive mistrust. All the way from Northallerton by Kumfi-Koach, and not really interested in our poet at all

2

except as the excuse for the trip: they would spend the afternoon comparing the Riddleford Woolys with the one at home, take the weight off their feet with a nice cup of tea and a Riddleford scone, and then it would be time to be getting back to Northallerton and father and the children.

Here and there I spotted members of a rare species — the true sightseers, the genuine pilgrims, the schoolmasters and civil servants who listen to Network Three whatever's on. They were not often to be seen in the light of open day: most of the time they were chivvying their wives and offspring down dark sidestreets to see things which the Official Guidebook doesn't mention but which are very much more worth seeing, really, than the things it does.

I was just getting clear of the Town Centre when a policeman held me up at a blinking zebra to let the first crocodile of the Season cross the street, taking its time, leaving a trail of sweetpapers and ticket-halves as though this was Hare and Hounds: pigtails swinging against jutting shoulderblades: shrieking, sniggering, sucking, giggling: tigerstriped blazer pockets crammed with postcards and Riddleford Rock and Presents From Riddleford. And all the while their poor perspiring shepherdess tried to parry the flow of inconvenient questions from Monica and Cynthia — 'But I didn't know he was *married* to Lady Jane, Miss Harris. . . . But how could he have children if he *wasn't* married, Miss Harris? . . . Can *anyone* have children, Miss Harris, even if they aren't married? . . . Miss Harris, could *you?*' The traffic surged forward again as the crocodile passed on its way, leaving the air heavy with the scent of Spangles.

Soon, I thought, as gradually I left behind me the bustle of the Town Centre — soon will the high midsummer pomps come on. Up will go the prices and down will come the standards, till we shan't be able to get a decent lunch for love or money. The pavements will be thronged thicker and thicker with rubbernecking trippers, the roads will be overrun with cars and coaches and cycles, and Riddleford will disappear beneath its summer coat of litter.

I felt a surge of resentment against these summer invaders. A quite unjustified resentment, for who was I to claim pride of ownership in Riddleford and Riddleford's poet, when I only came here first a twelvemonth back, and probably wouldn't stay here beyond the three years my scholarship at the Foundation had to run?

Yet somehow I did have this feeling of belonging.

Partly it was the result of working here at the Foundation, studying so closely the Life and Times of our poet. Partly it was my part-time job reporting for *The Riddleford Courant and Riddledale Advertiser*, poking my nose into anything and everything that happened hereabouts. Between the two it was hard not to feel I owned a stake in the town and in the town's poet — the left leg, say, or the liver and lights, like a medical student chipping in with the others to buy a corpse for dissection.

And I had been here out of season, too, when most of Riddleford is shut up for the winter. I had seen The Birth-place and Lady Jane's Cottage swept with sleet and heaped with snow. I had trodden the paths that *he* once trod in winter when only the doggedest pilgrims venture north. I had seen the cafés and restaurants shuttered and barred, the snowdrifts banked high against the gay boutique now bright with hand-knitted shawls and gaudy Riddleweave scarves. I had seen the bar of The Fox & Chicks empty of all but a few local regulars, I had seen Saint Bridget's congregation reduced to the handful of black-clad ladies who are her only true faithful.

And now that it was Spring again — now that Nicolas Grimsby had been brought out of his wrappers again for the trippers to drool over — it was hard not to feel myself part of a communal impresario.

II

Now once againe is come th' vneasie Spring,
That stirs the Pandarous Nightingale to sing,
Whose song to young Maydes' mindes doth fancies bring
To some of sleepe, to some of th' other thing . . .

SPRING in Riddledale is no doubt not too different today from Spring in Nicolas Grimsby's day, and no doubt it has much the same effect on the local fauna and, hence, on the female fancy. . . . It was easy to believe so this morning. Back in the High Street the new season showed itself in the return of the migrants — 'our friends from near and — er — far' as the Revd. Dwindle never fails to call them. But in the outskirts of Riddleford, Nature has it more her own way.

Here, life slows down and hushes. As I cycled out along the Carlisle Road — the trees thick with sticky buds against the hard blue windwashed sky, the hedges just coming to life again with their pale, pale green — I felt I had the Spring to myself. The only sounds were a mower mowing behind high hedges: a rake scratching through the gravel of someone's drive: a far-off cow mooing: and the passionate voice of an unseen windowcleaner telling me that he could have danced all night. Long after the top pops have been replaced in London, the melodies linger on in our backwater.

My first port of call on this morning's assignment for the *Courant* was Mrs Bunting's Christmas-card cottage, Deep Thatch.

Many visitors mistake the Bunting place for one of the Sights, and hunt feverishly for it in their guide-books: perhaps, they ask themselves, it's The Birthplace, or the Almshouses? But something about the outward appearance of the house warns them that they are wrong: where are the noticeboards, the lists of Rules & Regulations, the litter-bins and the stall for postcards and souvenirs? Deep Thatch may be just as old and certainly more picturesque than the real Sights: but it is much too tidy to really *be* one.

Indeed it's almost too well cared for: and the garden continues the same Christmas-card effect, for all the flowers seem to bloom at once in defiance of what it says on the packet — in defiance, one would imagine, of Nature herself.

I was not afraid that Mrs Bunting would not give me the story I'd been told to get. To get her opinion on anything is child's play: it's turning the tap off again that's a man's job. As the leading spirit on any number of Riddleford committees, Mrs Bunting holds as many firm opinions on as many subjects as a member of a TV discussion panel.

To look at she is short and rounded and everywhere at

once: whereas Harold, her husband, is vague and gangling and scarcely ever to be seen. How on earth they ever came together, and how having come together they decided to stay together, is one of Nature's mysteries. She declares publicly that she has no time for painting, least of all Harold's: while he is never to be found concerning himself with any of her bustling activities. Yet neither would ever be happy without the other, and their domestic life is a delicately-balanced state of coexistence.

Besides Mr and Mrs there is also, unaccountably, a daughter — Scrubby, age 12. But more of her later. Neither she nor her father was on display when I cycled up to the cottage: Scrubby presumably away at school, Harold painting or seeking inspiration or something.

I lowered myself off my bike into a turmoil of snapping jaws and excited paws. Mrs B breeds Afghans. 'Just pups — perfectly friendly!' she called from the house, but I stayed anxious till their mistress appeared at the porch and they bounded off to maul her instead.

She was wearing cherry slacks and a huge off-white fisherman's jersey — by its smears of paint I guessed it had started life as Harold's. Her feet flapped in clopperty sandals as she led the way through to the cheery chintzy sitting-room, snug as a pub's back parlour.

'Nice to see you, Geoff — long time no see. Business or pleasure?'

'Sort of business. Grasmere's idea. It's this thing in the *Observer*. . . .' I got that far before she interrupted me.

'Stop! If it's business, let's make ourselves comfy first. Sit you down.'

7

I looked for somewhere to sit on the vast sofa, awash with seed catalogues, Chairmen's Reports, Conservative litera-ture, letters to all sorts of people and from all sorts of people, invitations, leaflets, booklets, folders and anything that can possibly be obtained free by clipping out the attached coupon (no obligation!). 'It's all organised!' she shrieked, dashing forward as I made to shift some of it. 'I can lay my hands on every blessed thing — don't move a muscle or I'm done for!'

She cleared me a little oasis, shooing away a sleeping dog who promptly made his bed on another pile of papers. 'Now hold on a moment while I fix a drink.' She fixed a whopping pink gin which I didn't want at all at this time of morning but didn't dare to refuse. Drinking is a natural human function at Deep Thatch — just as natural as sleeping or eating, far more natural than sex. Mrs B had made a little nest for her behind in a litter of old municipal balance-sheets. 'And now to business, my dear. What for can I do you?'

I told her briefly what it was Mr Grasmere, my editor, had sent me out after: the opinion of various prominent residents on this article in yesterday's *Observer*. 'You haven't seen it?'

'Not a hope! Haven't caught up with last week's yet. Never get round to the Sundays till Thursday at the earliest — I always mean to catch up, but somehow I never manage it. Let's have a look — wait till I find my specs.'

She peered at the newspaper cutting I handed her. 'Oh, not *another* book on him — why can't they leave the poor fellow alone? *"New Light on Nicolas Grimsby"* — I'm sure he'd far rather be left in the dark: I know *I* would!

"*Grimsby of Riddleford? A New Evaluation. By Lemuel Nightly.*" Never heard of him. And why, I wonder, the question mark after Riddleford?'

I suggested she better read on.

' "*The Common Reader*" — that means me, I suppose — "*may justifiably look askance at any further accretion to the mounting accumulation of Grimsbiana in our libraries. Surely, he may exclaim, all has been said that needs to be said?*" — Hear, hear! — "*Any new thesis, he may well suspect, has been confected less from a genuine conviction than from lust after kudos.*" — Just what I'm always saying myself, only I don't use such fancy words. — "*However, this new work does seem to throw new light on Nicolas Grimsby. Dr Nightly's style is as ungainly as ever, his style as devoid of grace or coherence: but his subject-matter claims our attention and perhaps deserves our respect.*" — Hm, I wonder. . . . "*The careful argument leads us step by step to the conclusion that the Riddleford poet comes in fact from the neighbouring town of——*" What's this, Geoff? Oh really, this time they've gone *too* far! "*— from the neighbouring town of Grimwick.*" '

Mrs Bunting laid down her cutting for a moment. 'No, this is too much! He must be pulling our legs! Nobody could seriously suggest that Grimsby came from that dreadful place!'

She went on with her reading, but now there was a militant edge to her voice which made me uncomfortable. I hoped she wouldn't take her wrath out on me. ' "*At first sight such a proposition appears preposterous,*" — I'll say! — "*but closer study shows that this argument deserves to be taken in all seriousness. Whether it is ultimately tenable it is not for this column to say: other and more expert heads must determine. But*

9

whatever their verdict, it must be admitted that Dr Nightly's book is a significant and stimulating contribution to the literature of Nicolas Grimsby."'

Mrs Bunting handed my cutting back to me. 'What in the world is a respectable paper like the *Observer* doing taking notice of a piece of idiocy like that?'

'Well, there may be something in it.'

'Rot. How could there be? Grimsby *is* Riddleford. As well say there could be something in the suggestion that Dickens was a Frenchman. Everyone's always known that Nicolas was born in Riddleford, that he lived in Riddleford and that he died in Riddleford.'

'The reviewer seems fairly impressed by the book.'

'Hm. . . . What do you people think of this over at the Foundation?'

I said I hadn't been in there yet this morning. 'I can't imagine they'll take it very seriously. This sort of nonsense is always happening. But at the same time there is always the chance that one of these crackbrain theories may turn out not to be quite so crackbrain after all. Grimsby died — when was it? — three hundred odd years ago. He was pretty well forgotten right up till the time of the Grimsby Revival — he doesn't rate half a line, for instance, in Dr Johnson's *Lives of the Poets*. Well, think how much evidence may have been mislaid in all that time! Think of what they have turned up just in the last fifty years or so: the Willimoteswyke MS., the Unthank Bequest and all.'

My hostess made a rude face. 'But all this about his coming from Grimwick?'

'Oh,' I excused myself, 'I'm not saying this Dr Nightly can prove his case. I just wouldn't like to come out too strongly against him until I heard what he had to say.'

Mrs Bunting laughed. 'I suppose you scholars have to sit on the fence. But not me. If your Mr Grasmere wants my opinion, tell him I don't believe a word of it. . . . What would the sightseers say, coming all the way up to Riddleford only to find that Nicolas Grimsby never lived here at all?'

I reminded her that facts are facts, but she wasn't having any. 'Bunkum, Geoff. Facts are what you make 'em. Your Professor Bissentine — Bubbles, isn't that what you call him? — a clever man like him should be able to put this Nightly in his place.'

'Of course we'll do what we can. . . .'

'Of course you will. I didn't doubt it, my dear.' She rewarded me with a big motherly grin — the same, no doubt, which she uses to make her committees do what she wants them to do. Helen of Troy could have had nothing on Hilda Bunting whether in winning friends or influencing people, launching ships or burning topless towers.

She paused and waved her specs over her oceans of paper. 'All that bumf, Geoff — that's the life of Riddleford. It's a town with a lot of life in it. And it's all thanks to Nicolas, bless his randy old heart! We can't afford to lose him, Geoff! We have to defend him against the Nightlys of this world. . . .'

I scribbled into my notebook a few telling phrases that I could work up later into my story. Hilda Bunting was obviously very ready to take up arms against anyone who threatened her Nicolas.

The Afghans helped me away from the house with friendly encouragement. People on bicycles — errand boys, newspaper boys, postmen — were plainly fair game as far as they were concerned: and as I cycled down the gravel path, wobbling somewhat from the gin, they bounded beside me and stood barking at the gate until I was out of sight.

III

NEXT came Colonel Jonson-Platt.

I was distinctly nervous about tackling the Colonel. Ever since I did my military service anyone over the rank of First Lieutenant has always been vaguely associated in my mind with God. It was no use fixing my mind on the Colonel's droopy moustache and watery eyes: it was no use reminding myself that he was a political blimp and a mental fossil, who said damn silly things at public meetings and wrote damn silly letters to the long-suffering Editor of *The Times*. He was still to me a thunderbolt-happy Jupiter who might eat me if he chose.

What made me the more nervous was that I was now venturing to approach him on his own ground. Up till now I'd seen him only in one or other of his various public roles, playing a carefully prepared part as Pillar of the Riddleford Liberals, Master of the Riddledale Foxhounds, Chairman of the Riddleford Hospital Board, Churchwarden at Saint

Bridget's, President of the Riddleford Rugby Football
Club. But here was I intruding upon him at home, when he
had relaxed the set of his military shoulders, loosened his
collar, softened his army face to a fond father's, mellowed
his parade-ground bark to the genial gruffness of a loving
husband.

Nobody seemed to be in the house when I rang, not until
I tried a second and a third time: then a maid appeared who
told me I might perhaps find the Colonel round the back.
And so I did — emerging from a stable with his hands
dripping with blood.

He seemed in no way self-conscious about it, so I thought
it polite to pretend not to have noticed anything. What
business was it of mine, after all, if he had been doing in the
memsahib or flogging some impudent lackey within an
inch of his life? Instead I explained my errand, and he said
Surely, yes, he'd spare me a minute — just a minute, mind.
He led the way into the house wiping his hands on a silk
handkerchief, through back rooms full of mangles and
saddles and wellington boots.

Leaning back in one of the gun-room's deep black leather
chairs I felt as though I had walked into an illustration from
Country Life. My host sat in the chair opposite, reading the
Observer review twice through with no comment but a
muffled rumbling like a tube train burrowing into its tunnel.
I sipped the huge scotch that he had poured me and
awaited the explosion.

When it came, it came too fiercely for me to note down
more than a few key phrases in my notebook. Handing
back my cutting, he launched into a tremendous tirade
against what he called 'the bright boys' — of whom from

his description I appeared to be one, though he didn't hold it particularly against me.

'It's you clever lot who make all the trouble in the world, whether you mean it or no. You will have things black and white, that's the trouble with you: you must have things just so, neat and orderly — and of course that's where the bickering starts, because you *can't* have things just so, things weren't *meant* to be just so. . . . Mind you, I don't want you to think I'm in favour of anarchy. Of course I'm not. But there's such a thing as being *too* clever, of which this present business is, if I may say so, a pretty good example. Tell me, Mr Marston: d'you think this feller Nightly honestly cares a tuppenny cuss one way or t'other *where* Nicolas Grimsby lived, or even if he lived at all? I'm ready to wager he doesn't: I'm ready to wager he's just doing it to inflate his own beastly little ego — raising the question only so's he can strut and be admired for his cleverness!'

And so Colonel Jonson-Platt went on: and really I felt inclined to agree with him — in this comfortable armchair, with this fine liquor seeping into my bloodstream, I resented anyone who went stirring up things that had no need to be stirred up. . . . I leant back and let the Colonel's indignation flow on: I looked at the Colonel in polo kit on the wall, at the Colonel with his Cavalry Regiment, at the Colonel with his favourite hunter. And when the Colonel looked at me for a nod I nodded.

'However, all that apart, you tell Grasmere he can count on me. I don't know what a chap like meself can do: but what there is, tell him I'm ready to do it. Not, mark you, that I see all that you bright boys see in Grimsby's poetry.

14

Lots of it seems just plain lavatory stuff to me. . . . But there, I dare say I'm not quite so up-to-date as I should be.'

He clambered to his feet, and I drained the rest of my scotch and followed him. 'Now, if you'll excuse me — mare having a spot of trouble: got a youngster inside her don't seem especially anxious to emerge into this merry world of ours — don't know that I altogether blame it, eh?

'Anyway' — he gave me a bloody wave from the doorway — 'anyway, Grasmere can count on me. Grimsby's a Riddleford man, and that's the important thing when all's said and done, isn't it?'

IV

NEXT came the Rectory and the Rector's den. A heavy comfortable masculine room. French windows looked on to a lawn studded with late daffodils and battered croquet hoops that seemed to have been planted there for ever. . . . A room nostalgically reminiscent of the serene security of school and college. Everything it contained — the Cambridge-crested spill holder on the mantelshelf, the firescreen with the college colours, the crossed oars, the yellowing panoramas of undefeated cricket teams with Mr Dwindle aggressive and pre-Christian and strange — everything echoed the old values, the unchallenged principles. Sitting waiting while the housekeeper fetched the decanter and the biscuit barrel, I could have been in my old Headmaster's study: temporarily

I slipped back into a world where the ideal of *mens sana in corpore sano* still made sense.

'And how are things down at the Foundation?' asked the Rector, offering me one of those strange dry biscuits that Huntley & Palmer appear to manufacture exclusively for their country parson customers, which you could never buy in a chain store or a supermarket. 'Still too many scholars chasing too few facts?'

'That's about the size of it, sir.' I handed him the cutting. Mr Dwindle looked apprehensively at the streaks of blood left on it by the Colonel. 'Ha, what have we here?' he asked, perhaps thinking it must be some murder clue I was hoping he might identify. I think I disappointed him when I explained what my editor had sent me out to do.

He looked a little more closely at the scrap of newsprint and exclaimed, 'Oh, but I saw this yesterday! I made a note to ask Mrs Dwindle to order the book from Boots Library.'

'You think there may be something in it, sir?'

'Well, one must preserve an open mind, mustn't one? No need for me to tell you it is by no means the first occasion, though, that someone has had some such notion . . . let me see now. . . .' He ran a pointing finger along his shelves, reached down a massy blue and gold volume which I recognised as the *Oxford Companion to Grimsby Studies*.

'You people at the Foundation no doubt consider this book thoroughly out of date,' observed the Rector maliciously as he hunted for his reference. 'But I find it suffices for my modest requirements. . . . Aha yes, here we are. It was Stevens — another Oxford man, by the by — who first suggested that our Nicolas was no native of Riddleford. Though I see no reference here to Grimwick.'

'I take it, sir, that is Dr Nightly's contribution. He must have come across some new evidence.'

'We must wait and see, mustn't we, Geoffrey? But I doubt if Nicolas has any more to fear from the Nightlys of this world than Shakespeare from the Baconians. . . .'

He walked across to the french windows and gazed across the lawn and the intervening trees to the spire of Saint Bridget's ('A doubtless well-intentioned but characteristically clumsy addition by a late c.19 benefactor to the original E.E. fabric' — PEVSNER). 'I've grown accustomed, you know, to being Nicolas Grimsby's Rector. His spirit is so much a living thing still — you will perhaps think this whimsical — that I have come to feel for him as for one of my living parishioners. It is a privilege I should not care to lose after all these years.'

'I'm sure Dr Nightly will never prove his case, sir.'

'I trust not,' Mr Dwindle sighed, 'I trust not indeed. But these are deceptive times. What does Nicolas say? —

> *Our new Philosophers blacke out the Sun,*
> *Make Douting Thomases of euery one.*

It is hard to have faith and certainty in anything much. . . . Another glass of sherry? Another biscuit?'

With Mr Dwindle's sherry fighting it out with Mrs Bunting's gin and the Colonel's best whisky in my empty stomach, I was unsteadier than ever as I cycled away from the Rectory and back to the busy hurrying town again.

V

BEFORE I did my last piece of opinion-gathering I thought I had better call in at the *Courant* office in case there was anything new. I left my bike outside and climbed to the top of the tilting wooden stairs, shaken over the decades by the presses down below. I gently eased my way into our poky office on the top floor, looking out over the streets and shops of sunny Riddleford.

'Hullo, stranger!' sang out Gloria as I elbowed my way between the overcrowding filing cabinets. Gloria was our typist-secretary-switchboard besides doing any number of other things as well, from sticking stamps on our insurance cards to making small advances on next Friday's pay packet.

She was one of the Swanson Glorias, conceived in the year of *What a Widow!* and brought to birth while *Tonight or Never* was first showing. Her special interests were babies, the ballet and the Royal Family. In addition she had a restrained and utterly respectable 'thing' about Trevor Howard: several magazine photographs of him were gloyed on to the filing cabinet alongside the calendar from the Agricultural Suppliers and Seedsmen which showed two cardinals playing chess, and entitled 'Your move, your Eminence!'

Whether it was something in my walk or my talk, or a whiff of my breath as I passed her, I don't know: but 'My goodness!' Gloria exclaimed. 'We've got off to a good start this morning, haven't we!'

I gave her a cheerful grin and didn't answer.

'Oh, Geoff has champagne with his breakfast kippers every morning, don't you, Geoff!' This from young Alec, twentyish and learning the trade with desperate keenness. One day he would leave Northumberland for London and show those Fleet Street phonies a thing or two. In the meantime his rickety work-table, shuddering beneath his violently maltreated typewriter, was rather unkindly known to the rest of us as The City Desk.

The third desk was empty when I came in. It usually was. It belonged to Jim, our scruffy-minded but expert space-seller, who did his business not by telephoning from his desk but by telling filthy stories from pub to pub while he talked local tradespeople into advertising in our columns. The only time he was at his desk for more than five minutes at a time was when he was being Auntie Muriel of the Children's Page.

I never realised, till I came to work on the *Courant*, just how much blood, toil, tears and sweat goes into getting out a local paper once a week. Now I was learning fast. And the first thing I had learnt was the Golden Rule — Everything Has To Go In.

Everything — which means anything that is in any way the concern of the good people of Riddleford, and all in correct detail. My headline:

'RIDDLEFORD BOY WEDS RIDDLEFORD GIRL'

must be followed by a moment-to-moment account of the ceremony and an inch-by-inch description of the clothes worn, plus of course pictures of the blushing bride even if she's only the girl who sells baby powder all week at Timothy White's, and of the grinning groom even if most days he's heaving coke off Messrs. Rumbleby's truck.

Every prizewinner must be scrupulously named when I described the Riddledale Golf Club Whist Drive. I must reveal which of the stalwarts of the Riddleford Baptist Choir moved the gathering at the Chapel Social with her spirited rendition of *Just a Song at Twilight*. Last Saturday's match against Haltwhistle must be recounted faithfully — that was young Alec's job, and he had learnt to tactfully single out each individual member of the team for some award of praise. And so with the sheep market and the church bazaars, so with the christenings and the auctions, so with the tennis tournaments and the sheepdog trials, the Pony Club gymkhanas and the outings of the Girls' Friendly Society.

For the *Courant* has a trust to fulfil. The people of Riddleford don't care in the least what nonsense they read in their London newspapers: if the *Express* chooses to declare that there will be no war three days before war breaks out, they are not bothered. But it would be quite a different kettle of fish if Mr Grasmere were to tell them NO FLOOD DANGER IN RIDDLEDALE THIS YEAR and the Riddle subsequently overflowed — as it always overflows — its banks. No, the *Courant* has a trust to fulfil, and Mr Grasmere never allows us to forget it.

I sat down at my desk and contemplated its scratched and scarred top. The litter seemed to be exactly the same litter as I'd left earlier on. No urgent messages. No alarms and excursions. I felt relieved: all that gratuitous alcohol had unfitted me for serious activity.

'Oh, message from Jane,' Gloria called across the room. 'She said can you pick her up around six?'

'Can do,' I answered. 'Does she want me to call her?'

'Not if you can make it. She'll expect you.' Then, as I got to my feet again, she added 'Now where are you off to?'

'Haven't done with Dr Nightly yet. Still one more opinion to get — Joe Higgs.'

Gloria giggled and Alec gave a rude guffaw. 'Well, that beats the lot!' he cried. 'Any excuse to get inside The Fox & Chicks!'

'It's true!' I protested. 'Grasmere personally suggested Joe — "Must have the Voice of the People" were his very words.'

'Well, I don't know.' Alec shook his head despondently and turned his attention back to the Spring Cattle Sales. 'Some people get all the breaks.' He waved me a gloomy goodbye as I left.

On my way downstairs I passed Godfrey, our photographer. He too must have caught a whiff of my breath. 'My,' he commented wide-eyed. 'That's the sort of assignment I could handle. Can't you cut me in on it?'

VI

MOST of the Riddleford pubs have Grimsbified themselves from attic to cellar so that the tripper should
feel he is getting his money's worth. Souvenirs
are scattered high and low, scenes from The Plays take the
place of the customary Hunting Prints, convivial quotations
from The Works are carved on the imitation beams.

But The Fox & Chicks in Market Square doesn't pretend
to be anything but a place where you drink, just as Joe Higgs
himself doesn't pretend to be anything but a man who sells
you that drink. 'The Voice of the People,' Mr Grasmere
termed him: and fairly accurately, for if anyone is Sir Oracle
to the masses of Riddleford it's Joe. World politics? Champion marrows? Floodlit football? Whatever his customers
are talking about, Joe knows just that little more about it.
Nor is he ever shy to air that knowledge.

Today he drew a pint of his best bitter for me before he
would so much as glance at the *Observer* cutting. Then
'What's this, man?' he asked, wiping his hands on his cloth.

He read the review. 'Significant and stimulating, is it?
Well, man, me and the boys'll be happy to stimulate any
fellow comes marching in here trying to walk off with our
Grimsby. And you can tell Grasmere that with my compliments!'

'What seems to be the trouble, Joe?' said a new voice over
my shoulder. A heavy paw descended on my back. 'Hi,
Geoff boy,' the voice added.

'Gmorning, Mr Brandon,' said Joe.

Brandon Wayde sat himself down on the nearest stool. 'Well, looks like the faithful are swarming again,' he observed, jerking his head towards the tourist-thronged square outside, his big American voice making everyone else's soft Geordie tones sound like dwarfs tweetering. Joe pulled him a large bitter without being asked.

My attention was caught by a red, saffron and black thing knotted loosely round Brandon's neck. It looked as if it had been knitted by someone whose usual line was hearth-rugs. 'Nice tie,' I lied.

Brandon looked pleased: he told me he had found it in the Shawle Shoppe in the High Street.

'Nice,' I repeated. 'And I dare say it'll be a proud moment for you when the first Old Etonian comes up and shakes you by the hand and calls you brother.'

Brandon's hand darted to his neck in alarm. I think he'd have whipped it off there and then, but his eye caught mine and he relaxed. 'You lousy bastard,' he muttered, and stretched his hand for his beer.

But Brandon simply asked to be kidded about his dress. It was a long while before I figured out just what it was that made it so fascinating, but in the end I managed it. Brandon is, you might say, in mourning for the fact that he didn't fight in the Spanish Civil War — a deficiency from which a good many of Hemingway's countrymen seem to suffer. It does no good to point out that at the time of the fighting Brandon was a barefoot boy at school: the sense of guilt is still there, and his clothes still express that guilt.

Basically, no doubt, they conform with what the Well-Dressed American is wearing, just as basically his looks match the stereotyped young men in the *Esquire* fashion pages — men with the Rugged Look, the Casual Look, the Forward Look or wherever men are looking this year.

But just as there's a hint of individuality in his features suggesting that he doesn't go one hundred per cent along with the Americans' unquestioning devotion to group values, so Brandon's clothes are full of symbol and suggestion which sharply distinguish them from those of *Esquire's* campus playboys. Everything subtly suggests the guerilla, the fervent partisan of the International Brigade. The military-style trousers, the ex-army boots, the khaki shirt — all subconsciously conjures up the trenches before Salamanca, recalls the nostalgic camaraderie of those days which Brandon never knew, when one sat in tavernas with one's arms round the shoulders of other young lions, singing pink-tinged folksongs and swearing international brother-hood one with another, all gloriously one in the cause of — well, whatever it was.

Brandon laid the *Observer* cutting back on the bar counter. 'You trying to get rid of Grimsby for us, Geoff? This what the Foundation's driven you to?'

'Next thing you know, man,' Joe observed knowingly, 'they'll be wanting to dig up his tomb, make out his plays were written by that Marlowe.'

'You'd best get in first with a book to prove it, Joe.'

'I might at that!'

I thought I better bring the conversation to where Mr Grasmere wanted it. 'Could make a difference, couldn't it, Joe, if this Dr Nightly proved what he claims?'

'To me, you mean?'

'Yes. All these tourists. If you lost their custom I dare say it would make a tidy hole in your turnover?'

Joe thought this over as he sloshed a Wettex up and down the zinc bar. 'Ah, I don't think we could well do without them.' He looked round and saw no call to lower his voice. 'Noisy untidy lot, most of 'em. But we couldn't do without their money, that we couldn't.'

Just then he was called down the counter to look after another customer. 'Know what I think?' Brandon asked. 'I think Riddleford would be better off *without* Grimsby.'

'Even after what you've just heard?'

'Yes, even if it meant going back to being a one-horse market town. All the spivs making easy dollars out of the tourist suckers. . . . If Grimsby hadn't been born here, Riddleford might have had the chance to be itself. As it is, it's just one huge Grimsby racket, smothering the town in the fog of its own self-advertisement.'

I laughed. 'Now you make it sound as if it's *you* who wants to abandon Grimsby!'

'Oh, the harm's done now, Riddleford's committed to Grimsby and there's no helping it. I know I wouldn't like the job of persuading the good people of this town to let both the cash *and* the credit go.'

'Yes, it's certainly one or the other with all of them. I've been touting this cutting round some of our leading citizenry this morning, getting their views on it for the *Courant*.'

'Oh — who did you see? Mrs Bunting for one, I'll be bound?'

'Mrs Bunting, of course. She never reads a line of Grimsby, but she loves Riddleford and it follows naturally

25

that she must love Grimsby too. Then Colonel Jonson-Platt: he's doubtful whether Grimsby's really fit for family consumption — but the poet's a Riddleford man, so that puts him in the clear.

'Then the Rector; he's pleased as Punch that he's Rector of Grimsby's home parish, with *his* carcase rotting in the churchyard and *his* memorial gleaming in the church. And then there's Joe,' I added, smiling at the landlord who'd rejoined us and was polishing glasses with a towel which said 'Be An Angel And Dry Up'. 'There's Joe, and thousands like him. They just need the money the tourist trade brings them.'

Joe looked hurt. 'Now, man, there's more to it than that. I'm not denying, we like the trade the tourists bring us. But Grimsby, now: we're *proud* of him. We do have our pride, y'know, even if some of the time it don't show much. And if someone's going to come along and try to walk off with our Grimsby, he'll have us to reckon with before he does it.'

'You better let me quote you in the *Courant*, Joe!'

'You can do that, Geoff, and with pleasure.'

We ordered and ate some sandwiches and drank some more beer, and then I suggested a game of bar billiards.

'Hey, have we the time?' asked Brandon. 'We have a seminar at two, don't forget!'

'So we have! What is it this time?'

'The usual. Whatever it was last week continued in our next. The formative influences of somebody on something.'

'Well, it's close on two now — we better hurry.' We downed our drinks hastily, called goodbye to Joe, and hurried across the Market Square and into the Grimsby Foundation.

VII

N ICOLAS himself had none too flattering an opinion of us scholars:

> *What's a Scholler? One*
> *Who takes a candle to seeke out the Sun.*
> *Who holds all things created onely meant*
> *To furnish Themes for wrangling Argument.*

Heaven alone knows what he would say if he could set eyes on the Grimsby Foundation. Here in his own home town, practically on the doorstep of his Birthplace, an establishment created for the unique purpose of illuminating by research and conjecture the Life and Times of — Himself! How he would have jeered: how he would have wept!

The Foundation is housed in a largish building looking out over the Market Square. You can tell it is a beautiful building because it has

1 6 3 4

carved over the front porch. No doubt its original builders thought it attractive. Tourists today admire the dome erected on the roof by a stargazing contemporary of

Grimsby's, but it hardly improves the classic proportions. Nor is the integrity of the design aided by the Gothick turrets and wrought-iron fancy-work added in the eighteenth century by some Northumbrian hanger-on of the back-to-the-Romanticks movement.

Further excrescences were added by the Victorian owner, a lady novelist whose provocative three-deckers were in constant demand under the counter at Mudie's Circulating Library, and who was supposed by the locals to hold orgies — *unspeakable* orgies — in the West Wing which she herself added, lancing it with stained-glass windows depicting in a moody but disappointingly decorous manner the Rape of Lucretia.

All in all it is hardly surprising that, faced with this hodge-podge, the twentieth century has done little to the building beyond encouraging the virginia creeper to cover it as fast as it can.

The building has belonged to the Grimsby Foundation ever since Mr Omar Krankel, our founder, thought a Grimsby Foundation would be a good idea. That was back in 1937: and the establishment had scarcely time to get started before the war dumped the military on the doorstep. I don't know what they used it for, but it must have been something fairly hectic to judge from the traces they left behind them.

It was not until after the war that the Foundation really got off to a proper start. A couple of dozen students — half of them American, the rest international — were lured by the offer of scholarships to Riddleford. Brandon was one of the American contingent: I was one of the others.

VIII

THE two of us now squeezed into the Seminar Room as softly as might be, heads down like ostriches, hoping nobody would see.

'. . . this question of Anez Guck, bless her heart.' Professor Bissentine completed his sentence, then peered over at us across the top of his pince-nez. 'Mr Marston — Mr Wayde . . . I had better explain for your benefit what I have already explained to everyone else. We are considering Anez Guck. Is either of you acquainted with the lady in question, might I ask?'

The name meant nothing to me. I guessed she was yet another transatlantic scholar who, under the friendly auspices of the University of Poughkeepsie, had proved with the help of numerous appendices and coloured graphs that Grimsby's source-material was derived from some newly-unearthed pagan fertility rituals, not otherwise encountered outside New Mexico.

'You have nothing to help us? A pity. A great pity. For we, alas, are in scarce happier plight. We had cherished hopes — vainly, as it now transpires — that such scholarly minds as yours might draw from their treasure-houses of knowledge just the information we lacked. Alas, it seems it was not to be. . . .

'However,' he turned to face the other students, seated round the white oak refectory table, 'however, there does seem to exist a prima facie case for believing that she is the young person — I believe that is still the customary phrase — whereby our young poet had at any rate one of his illegitimate offspring.'

The students gazed at Bubbles, ballpoints poised, dumb. One of the Americans sneezed into a Kleenex just as the Professor was about to speak again. 'Your pardon,' he muttered. Bubbles paused heavily, then began again: 'If we can show that this Mistress Guck . . .' (he held up one of the familiar filing cards, a blue one, in his left hand) 'is one and the same as this Phyllis Guck, mentioned in Hardhand's *Galaxie of Gladsome Gems* . . .' (and he glanced at a similar but pink card held in his right hand) 'then there is some evidence for our little hypothesis. And it would be reassuring to be informed for certain about this unusual — well, no, not perhaps unusual: shall we say "quaint"? — this *quaint* episode in the career of our poet.'

His spectacled eyes panned slowly round us all, leering. I wanted to leer back but didn't dare.

Brandon leant across and handed me a slip of paper. Covertly I read it:

> *The case for believing it Grimsby*
> *Appears to be frightfully flimsby,*
> > *For no-one would have intimate relations with*
> > *A lady named Guck*
> *Except in a moment of whimsby.*

I giggled. Bubbles peered over at me suspiciously, and I longed to do something to prick his pomposity. . . . How he adored those precious slices of pasteboard, sole tangible results of the work we did here under his wing. Here we all

were, dredging among the backwaters of Grimsby's Life-
and-Times, and all we had to show for it was a shelf-ful of
Ph.D dissertations and an occasional truculent contribution,
unpaid for, to a learned quarterly. But these cards of
Bubbles' were different. They were the actual evidence
which vouched for the actual activity of this actual Foundation.

Every now and again, therefore, the authorities — a
euphemism for Bubbles himself — gave birth to a Concept.
During several days this Concept matured in the minds of
the Faculty, then it was waved before the eyes of the Student
Body until by sheer manhandling it was licked into a Project. Upon which a starting signal was given and we all
flailed into dusty library shelves, flicked through furlong
after furlong of microfilm, till we had stacked up another
drawer-full of coloured cards, each with its little crumb of
lore about His Life, His Times.

And if, as I'm afraid did sometimes happen, the results of
our Project were so trivial that even Bubbles had to admit
their insignificance, why, even so they had been valuable
discipline. We had had the chance to use the tools of our
trade. We had enjoyed the opportunity to conduct the kind
of pure, disinterested, *clean* research, untouched by human
hands and unsullied by earthy practical considerations,
which was what Bubbles loved more than anything else in
this world.

But, in a different way, he loved too the tangible results.
He loved the little bits of yellow, blue or orange pasteboard
we produced for him — for they, and they alone, excused
this Foundation and justified him to Mr Krankel across the
ocean.

Now Bubbles stroked his two slices of card between finger and thumb as he leant forward and peered round the room. 'Now who, I wonder, would care to check up the facts of this affair for us? It would involve running into Carlisle from time to time to consult the Archives, of course. But otherwise I don't see that it need take up too much of anyone's valuable time.'

His wandering gaze was brought to a standstill by a scribbling girl student bent over an enormous notebook written in blue and red and green with unbelievable neatness and devotion. 'Ah, Miss Stuart-Stotts! I think perhaps *you* might find this not altogether without interest.'

Phoebe Stuart-Stotts looked up, brushed the hair off the top of her forehead, and glared at Bubbles.

Bubbles beamed back in return.

'Very well, Professor,' she replied sharply, and immediately returned to her writing again — her notebooks in which was recorded everything that had been thought and said about Grimsby, in glorious Technicolor, for the future delectation of the young daughters of the Social Register in Denver, Colorado.

'Trust the old lecher to give something juicy to one of the girls,' Brandon whispered. Particularly, I thought, Phoebe — poor frustrated Phoebe.

Bubbles caught the echo of Brandon's whisper: 'Ah, Mr Wayde: you have something to contribute?'

Brandon hastily improvised. 'It just crossed my mind, Professor, perhaps Bresson said something about this matter?'

'Ah yes, thank you, a point, Mr Wayde, a point indeed.

But I'm afraid — yes, very much afraid — that my dear old friend Bresson avoids the subject altogether. Far be it from me to suggest why, but such is alas the case. Indeed I rather fear the whole affair is quite untouched — *virgo intacta*, you might say.'

He smiled and paused a moment. Then 'Except of course by myself. I seem to recall touching — oh, very briefly — upon the subject in one of my books: the one on Philip Rossiter, I fancy. There was something of a parallel there. Has anyone, I wonder, chanced to skim through my little book on Rossiter?'

Silence.

Bubbles loved that silence. He positively revelled in our collective embarrassment.

'Ah well, pity. But it's quite out of print, or so my publishers tell me. Quite sold out. But we really should try to get hold of a copy for the library here — not naturally for you people to read, but for me to refer to. I have not even a copy of my own — I gave my last copy away, I remember, one of my students begged it off me and I lacked the heart to refuse. . . . Still, Miss Stuart-Stotts, don't you think there is something rather fascinating about blazing a trail, setting foot where no man has gone before? You will be able to tell us whether or not this affair is connected, as I believe it is, with his poem *Love's Regrets*. You remember the opening lines . . .'

His voice dropped half an octave to his reciting voice, so that for a moment we seemed to hear not the flesh-and-blood director of the Foundation, smug and silly, but the disembodied personality we had heard so often on the Third, the world-renowned scholar speaking from Olympian heights cloud-high above our particular level of the Groves of Academe.

> *'How like a Poyson is this Draught of Loue,*
> *How sourelie sweete it lyeth on the Tunge,*
> *How sudenlie it gripeth on the Heart. . . .*

It is no uncommon thing, Miss Stuart-Stotts, for a man to feel remorse after making physical love to a woman. *Post coitum triste* — yes, the Ancients had their phrase for it, and I dare say today's trick cyclists could tell you a deal more. However stifled he may be by the trappings of this neo-matriarchal civilisation of ours, a man cannot avoid something of the agenbite of inwit when he has had truck with the Female Principle. Our young scapegrace was, I fancy, suffering from a twinge of just this atavistic ailment when he penned these lines.

'Remember,' he continued, staring at Phoebe so intently that she was compelled to leave off scratching with her pens and to look back at him, 'remember, Miss Stuart-Stotts, if you can sort anything for us out of this troubled business, you will be making an original contribution to our knowledge of the period. It is unfortunate, I admit, that some of the bypaths of history should lead us into somewhat unsavoury fields. But we must bear with that for their sake who come after. They, I feel sure, will count themselves our debtors. . . . Remember, Miss Stuart-Stotts, remember, all of you: it's not what *you* want to know, it's not what *I* want to know. It's what *the world* wants to know!'

He paused and peered round at us over his glasses. 'I hope we all of us realise that, eh?' Nobody stirred. He caught my eye for a flash, his travelling eye caught every eye in turn. 'That is what our Foundation is for.' Somebody coughed. 'As you know.'

He was silent, and there was an after-sermon feeling in the Seminar Room, as if we should all feel we had been done good to. Slowly the tension relaxed.

'There is one other small matter that I must touch on. A triviality, but I suppose we ought not to ignore it. I have a pamphlet here — a pamphlet, I call it, because it does not really deserve the title of "book" despite the fact that its publishers seem for some reason best known to themselves to assess its worth at five and thirty silver shillings.'

The book was held up for us all to see. 'I think we should all of us try to read this book. Not, let me hasten to point out, not because it is great, or even because it is good. But because it is an admirable example of the absurdities to which misguided scholarship can descend.'

'What's it about, Professor?'

'I should like very much to know myself.'

'You mean you haven't read it, sir?'

'Why, yes, I have read it. But I fear I am still in the dark. Perhaps I shall understand better when some of you people have read it too. With your youthful, active brains perhaps you will be better able than I to disentangle the author's meaning. If he has one, that is.'

He threw the book down on to the table and left the room.

One of the American girls owned up to having already read the book. 'Some crazy mixed-up prof,' she commented with distaste, 'claims Grimsby didn't live in Riddleford at all. How d'you like that?'

'Thought people had got over trying to peddle that sort of crap!'

'Molly, tell us the truth now — is it really required reading?'

'You heard what the Professor said, didn't you?'

'That's your friend Nightly's book, isn't it?' Brandon asked me.

I picked up *A New Evaluation* and flipped through the pages. It had the usual dreary dryasdust appearance which university presses invariably give to the most revolutionary of subversive theories.

'No peeking at the last page to see whodunit!' someone exclaimed. 'Play fair and read it from start to finish like a man!'

'Maybe *Reader's Digest* runs a condensed version?' someone hopefully suggested.

'Me, I'll wait till they get out a film of the book. Then I'll read the book of the film of the book.'

'Anyone coming for tea?'

Another merry seminar was over.

IX

WHILE the rest of the crowd headed for one or other of the hundred and one dainty teashops that line the streets of Riddleford, I ducked back to the *Courant* office to get my piece sorted out. I put in a couple of hours bashing at the battleship-type typewriter, built in the days when secretaries were easy to come by and why shouldn't they break their backs?

When I had got it all knocked into some kind of shape I paper-clipped it all together and put it into the correct maroon folder. Mr Grasmere wasn't in his editorial sanctum sanctorum so I dropped it into his IN-tray. There would be plenty of things the matter with it: I was still a mere apprentice so far as the taboos and sacred cows of local affairs were concerned. But that would wait till the morning.

Gloria was powdering her nose ready to meet her boy-friend: Alec was still up to the neck in columns of figures and looked as if he would be here all night. The office clock said it was getting on for six, so I draped the cover over my machine, said goodnight to the others, ran down-stairs, and walked across to The Clay & Wattle to pick up Jane.

The Clay & Wattle is not as genteel as The Lady Jane Tea Rooms, where they dish out Earl Grey and toasted tea-cakes which you eat with those half-knife half-fork implements, delicately surrounded by the same old ladies who buy those knobbly hand-knit stoles from Raggity Pam's, the hand-knit stole shop. Nor on the other hand is it so brutally efficient as Slosh Jenkins' Dew Drop Inn Snax Bar, where you can stuff down hamburgers and espresso with the teds till the small hours. But there are enough distractions to keep your mind off the food which, after an initial burst of gastronomic adventurousness when the menu offered goulashes and risottos, moussakas and baklava, relapsed into the usual choice of egg and chips, plaice and chips, sausage or beans or anything else and chips, which is what nine out of ten of our visitors honestly prefer.

Bill and his sister Shelagh who run The Clay & Wattle might have dressed it like any other café if Bill had not had his fatal inspiration. But he did: and now it's too late. The inspiration went to his head and Shelagh's too, and there is nothing to be done. Their café is, now and forever, the world's most olde worlde café.

The Clay & Wattle is all that the tripperiest tripper could sigh for. As you step in off the pavement you bang your head, unless you are extra-careful or a dwarf — they had the doorway specially lowered on purpose. 'Softens 'em up!' Bill says. Then down a pair of slippery steps on to the floor — highly polished oak with little furry rugs: crossing the café is like negotiating a frozen river by jumping from ice-floe to ice-floe.

You sit at a clumsy wooden table built by someone who had an allergy to right angles. You bark your shins at an unexpected jut of wood. You lean back in your mock wheelback chair and scrape the skin off your shoulder-blades. You look round at the walls — an unmatched collection of objets d'art bears triumphant witness to Shelagh's obsession with local auctions. Views of irrelevant cathedrals; ancient maps of distant counties; horse brasses; warming pans; quotations from Grimsby done on wood with a hot poker. The windows are leaded, diamond-paned, coloured yellow and pink. Interspersed are panes of bottle-glass. For illumination you get genuine candlelight — expensive, but a sure hit with the customers. It flares and gutters all over the place and combines with the fire — one of those imitation-log devices flickering with real electricity — to suggest The Bandits' Cave in a romantic operetta. Tea in The Clay & Wattle is an Experience.

What with the alarming décor and the uninspiring fare, there might not seem to be much incentive for civilised people to patronise The Clay & Wattle. But it does boast one other distinctive feature. It has Jane.

Jane came to The Clay & Wattle only as a temporary help, just after leaving college, to try to earn a bit of pocket money one summer. Ever since then she's always been on the verge of leaving — oh, any day, really: but she still hasn't.

She came at a time when she was at a loose end, and was attracted by an unusual ad in the Sits Vac column:

> OLDE-FANGLED TEA-SHOPPE requires newfangled waitress. Experience and brains not essential, but good looks and good temper vital. Wages just bearable. Apply &c.

Now that I know Bill I can see that it was just the advertisement he would have concocted. He and Shelagh fell for Jane straight away, and she fell for them. In next to no time she had become one of the family instead of a hired skiv and was installed in an attic flatlet in their own house, about ten minutes' walk from the High Street. Her family thought as families do that she really ought to be giving some Serious Thought to her Future and her Prospects and her Career, and were rather inclined to disapprove: but she told them she might as well be earning while she made up her mind what she wanted to do with herself, and they could hardly quarrel with that.

To passers-by The Clay & Wattle looks an oasis of pseudo-period calm. But behind the 'Staff Only' door you are back in the jungle — the chef and the pastrycook and Jane and the washer-upper all falling over each other among the steaming coffee-machines, the mechanical bean-shredders, the whirring mixers and the 'Autochip' patented fryer.

Bill and Shelagh reckon to cater for all who come, so into The Clay & Wattle come the Mothers' Union outings and the icecream-sucking cyclists, the schoolmasters with their children, and the children with their whining and their perpetual longing to visit the toilet. Americans come in and surround the table with their cameras, guide books, raincoats, bags, glasses, souvenirs, maps, hats and offspring, and are rather slow in the uptake about what they want to eat. Know-all hard-faced ladies demand a 'Devon' tea and point out acidly that in Ilfracombe you aren't fobbed off with 'Kreama' mock-cream substitute.

All very exhausting. But Jane handles her job very nicely. Somehow she always manages to look charming even if she's only threading her way between overcrowded tables with a Mixed Grill in one hand and a Dover Sole in the other, smiling at the lady at table 13 who wants some more hot water and the Frenchman at No. 5 who is complaining that he cannot understand the menu (written in School Certificate French by Shelagh) — all on a blazing summer's afternoon, when sensible people are siesta-ing, after three sittings of lunch have come and gone and the place is still packed and she hasn't had her own lunch yet and they should be laying the places for tea. . . .

X

JANE was waiting for me, already changed out of her waitress's pinny, tidied and transformed into a girl again.

'Nice seminar, darling?' she asked, waving goodnight to Bill and Shelagh as we left the tea-shop.

'The usual.'

'No startling contributions to Eng. Lit.?'

'What d'you think?'

'Honestly, I don't know what you people do with yourselves — using the taxpayers' money just to sit and natter!'

'It's not the taxpayer's money, it's Mr Krankel's.'

'Well, if I was Mr Krankel I'd be jolly fed up with the way my money was being wasted! Doesn't he ever pop across and see how his beloved Foundation is getting on?'

'Never that I've heard of.'

'I would if I was him, if I'd spent all that money.' Jane looked about her and noticed the way we were walking. 'I thought we were going to your place?'

'So we are, but I've got to pick up my bike from The Fox & Chicks.'

'What were you doing there?' she pounced. 'In fact where've you been all day? When I tried to phone you, Gloria said you were out on a Special Assignment. Sounds like a serial on TV — was it?'

I told her all about my morning's work. 'Ooh!' she said, her wide brown eyes wider than ever. She thought for a moment, then went on, 'But somebody's always trying on something like that, aren't they? What about that Swede who said that the writing on the Memorial proved that it was Shakespeare or someone who *really* wrote Grimsby's poems? Whatever became of him?'

'I suppose he left with his tail between his legs. I imagine people like him simply switch to some other project, like we do at the Foundation — start proving that Lady Hamilton was really Marie Walewska, with an appendix on her vital statistics.'

Jane giggled politely. 'But you don't think this Dr Nightly is going to turn out to be anything exciting, do you?'

'You never know. He doesn't have to actually prove his case, you know, to make quite a nuisance of himself. All he needs is to sow the occasional seed of doubt among the tourists. A panic starts — and bang goes Riddleford's livelihood!'

'And bang go our jobs too! . . . But why would he want to do that?'

'Don't ask me,' I said. 'Why do any of these people want to prove the things they try to prove? They aren't bothered by the results of their research — they're only interested in facts. Or supposed to be, anyway.'

'I don't know that it would matter, anyway. Riddleford would still be just as nice a place, even without Grimsby. Besides, I've always thought most of The Legend was phoney. I mean, does anybody seriously believe all that about The Birthplace — that little Nicky's feet *really* pattered up those wooden stairs, or that he was *truly* born just where the Curator says he was?'

'Most of the trippers believe it, darling, and that's what matters. There's just enough evidence for them to feel happy about pulling the wool over their own eyes. If this Nightly fellow pulls it off again, it'll all be over. It won't do any good to say that Riddleford would be just as nice without Grimsby. Think of fake pictures: how annoyed people get when they fork out thousands for a Vermeer and it turns out to be a Van Meegeren. The painting's just as good, but you try and tell them so!'

'But what's the point in their coming here at all, Geoff? They don't really care about Nicolas. They think they do while they're here, and if they are lucky the effect lasts a day or two, and they make a resolution to read the plays aloud together by the fireside, all cosy like, every evening. And what happens? Up comes something on the telly they simply mustn't miss, and the good resolution crumbles, and back goes the Collected Grimsby into the glass-fronted bookcase, and only a "Present from Riddleford" bookmark to witness to their good intention!'

I agreed, laughing, but didn't reply anything. Instead I

looked at the passers-by as we moved through them. The tourists weren't so thick on the ground now. A good many would have cycled or driven away or trained home with the return half of their day tickets. Some would be among the potted ferns of their hotel lounges, writing piles of post-cards and sucking the ends of their pens as they tried to say something different on each, even though each was ad-dressed to someone different. Others would be dressing for the Riddlemarket Theatre, where the posters announced that tonight the Grimsby Players were presenting *The Faithless Friend*.

As I looked at the few who were still about, finishing the rolls of film in their cameras by sunsetlight because they were leaving first thing in the morning, I thought that though what Jane had said was somewhat cheerless, I couldn't deny it was probably true. 'Well, anyway,' I said, 'we can at least see that Grimsby is preserved for Riddleford.'

But she had an answer to that too. 'Pet, you're just too head-in-the-clouds for this day and age! D'you really think the people of Riddleford care more for Grimsby than the trippers do? I expect Mr Dwindle really loves him, and sits in his study in the evenings reading him for pleasure. But I bet he's the only person in the whole of Riddleford who does!'

There were still plenty of Riddleford natives about as we walked towards Market Square. The shopkeepers were putting up their shutters with a rattle and bang. The errand boys had put away their aprons and were city slickers again, gathered on the sidewalks outside the record shops which kept open for them, and from whose doors came the foot-tapping voice of Tommy Steele or the head-nodding beat of Basie. The shopgirls were cycling home, turning their head-scarved necks for a last 'Ta-ta till morning!' and tossing their heads at the teddy boys' whistles.

The last housewives were off home with their shopping bags full, another raid on the shops successfully carried out. They certainly didn't look as if they had much poetry in their souls. They shambled along, dressed in their various combinations of brown, fawn and beige, with occasional daring dashes into green — some of them ponderously alone, others complaining to each other in long whining periods like model aeroplanes in flight or crisply chitter-chattering like cornflakes. They waddled to the concrete bus-shelter and stood, stolid and dull, with carriers full of Domestos and pilchards and earthy vegetables, waiting till buses came to chug them to the outskirts of the town.

> The gadding Many in
> Their blinkers hie
> Nor do descrie
> Beyond the Shelle and Skinne

said Nicolas. Housewives can't have altered much since his day.

We turned the corner into Market Square. 'Well, you've got to admit, *somebody* likes Grimsby!' I remarked. We both looked to where in the centre of the Square stood the 'American' Statue, presented in 1907 as the inscription tells us by Mr Joseph Himmelburger, a brewer of Houston, Texas.

After The Birthplace the American Statue is the most-photographed edifice in Riddleford. It represents the infant

Nicolas being suckled (very discreetly) by his mother: beside them, one of the Muses holds up a scroll on which is inscribed one of the few chaste poems he was to write in later years. I once overheard a pair of trippers as they stood gazing up at the American Statue in awed wonderment. Two cameras clicked as one, and then the girl said to her companion, 'D'you know, I wonder if it could be meant to be kinda symbolical?'

Our quaint American cousins approach the statue with the same veneration that they have for genuine relics like the Grimsby Family Bible or the Parish Register where it says when Nicolas died. The English, too, show their appreciation of Mr Himmelburger, but they confine it to November the Fifth, when at least one of the Riddleford Guys is regularly named for the generous Texan.

'I like Americans. At least they're enthusiastic,' said Jane. 'I like Mr Joseph Himmelburger.'

'So do I. I like all brewers on principle.'

'The trouble with you, pet, is you have no soul.'

'I expect the academic life has worn it away.'

'I shouldn't be surprised.'

At The Fox & Chicks my bike was leaning against the wall, waiting like a well-trained dog. Wheeling it along the pavement we walked back towards the river along the by now lamplit High Street. Past The Goose Arms — a particularly genuine and particularly pricey hotel. Past Lloyds Bank in mock Tudor and Boots in mock Tudor and Smiths in mock Tudor and only Woolworths daring to be itself in uncompromising red and gold. A slight breeze of evening swung the wrought-iron signs outside the chemist's, the shawl shop and the souvenir shop.

Outside this last we stopped to play Jane's Game. The object of this home-made sport was to see how many things we could spot in the window with *A Present from Riddleford* on it. The number to choose from is tremendous. The entire shop is full of useless objects which visitors are nevertheless happy to purchase — souvenir ashtrays, souvenir butter-knives, souvenir tea-strainers, bottle-openers, shopping list holders, comb-cases, paper-cutters, cigar-piercers, gadgets for decapitating eggs. There are table mats with pictures of The Birthplace and wineglasses embellished with The Goose coat of arms. There are india-paper editions of The Works in all manner of fancy bindings short of human skin. Hanging cards bearing Thoughts From Grimsby. All kinds of cigarette-boxes each with its own cunning mechanism to flip your cigarette up at you, untouched by hand and only slightly crushed about the middle. There are yacht-shaped table lamps, there are dog-shaped bookends, there are pottery gnomes for the garden pool and pottery birds in flights of three for the sitting-room wall. Clever dolls capable of all sorts of intimate functions. Model galleons to remind us we are a nation of seafarers. Models of horses and hounds to remind us we are a nation of animal-lovers. Passe-partout texts saying GOD BLESS OUR MORTGAGED HOME to remind us of our national sense of humour. And row on row of Toby jugs.

'Oh, these people! They don't deserve to have Nicolas at all!' Jane tugged me away from the window. 'Come along home before I'm sick!'

We walked in silence along the rest of the High Street, and turned into Mafeking Gardens when the last shops had been passed — where the sodium streetlights came to a stop and the softer gaslamps spread small, friendly pools of light at intervals. The sounds of the town died away altogether. Life here went on behind drawn curtains, within the dark silhouettes of the semi-detacheds, each with its tracery of aerial black against the purple sky, jutting out like a chameleon's tongue to draw mental sustenance from the ether. We passed Holmdene and The Laurels and Woolacombe and Deneholme and Briar Thorns and Dunromin . . . and so we came to my place.

XI

M Y place doesn't have a name like Deneholme or Dunromin: I am simply care of Miss Williams, though everyone knows that she herself lives the other side of town and that I rent the cottage from her.

House agents would call the cottage 'a bijou gem', and it has one extra advantage in that Miss Williams never disturbs me, which is just as well because she might not care for some of the liberties I've taken. For instance, there are the paintings which I felt obliged to take down: scenes of bazaar life in nineteenth-century Turkey by my landlady's great-uncle Hugo Williams, the well-known painter of scenes of bazaar life in nineteenth-century Turkey.

And then there are the texts. When I moved in the cottage was wellnigh wallpapered with texts: moral exhortations reproached me wherever I looked — not only in the bedroom, where perhaps one might forgive them, but in living-room, pantry, hall and kitchen too. Worst of all, Miss Williams' missionary zeal overflowed even into the bathroom. Several books had been left there, each with a passage selected for every day of the year — chosen one by a Methodist Army Chaplain, one by a Mother Superior, a third by a popular TV personality. Bored with the bath — if you're the sort of person who *can* be bored with the bath — you could stretch out a soapy hand for *The Moving Finger* and meditate steamily on the unaccountable ways Providence chooses to accomplish its ends. Assailed by constipation you could relieve the tedium with *In Green Pastures* — whose author saw God particularly in Nature, giving one a feeling of oneness with the vegetable world quite medicinal in its effect.

Each morning I opened my eyes on a card which said:

> **Who riseth first**
> **Seeth all things best**

which, as Brandon points out, is worse than a lousy rhyme: it simply isn't true.

But such an objection is mere sophistry in Mafeking Gardens. Here the Uncomfortable is equated with the Good: here 'Short-cut' is a dirty word, and no life is thought virtuous unless it is knobbly and uninviting from start to finish. My neighbours wake in the morning inwardly declaiming 'Let us then be up and doing!' and they forthwith up and do. The effort leaves them so exhausted that by nightfall they are fit for nothing but dozing dolefully before the flickering telly.

Mafeking Gardens means the women of Mafeking Gardens really, their menfolk being little better than lodgers who spend most of their days, understandably, away at work or the allotment or the pub. On the faces of the menfolk one detects, in sudden glimpses, a slinking discontent; but never on their wives'. As the womenfolk sink back in their Kumfi-Vue TV Lounge Suite, the mortgage on the house ticking off like clockwork, hubbie stacked ten foot deep in insurance, the instalments flowing smoothly for the washing-machine and the spindrier and the baby Austin, how could life be richer?

They have still not lost the habit of complaining over the garden fence, of course: but the grumbling is a polite act tactfully assumed to appease the neighbours, to avert the anger of the household gods from their smug hubris. Inwardly they are perfectly happy with their lives, luxuriating in their possessions and wallowing vicariously in Hollywood Gossip, advertisers' pipedreams and the plugged Top Ten.

What the women of Mafeking Gardens think of me in return I can only imagine. Every time I walk up my road the edges of the lace curtains are drawn back discreetly so that my neighbours can check on what I'm up to now. 'It seems to me I'm perfectly normal,' I protested to Jane. 'I haven't turned Miss Williams' cottage into a disorderly house. I don't run out into Mafeking Gardens with no clothes on or undress in front of an open window. I go out shopping just the way they do, and come home with packets of Shredded Wheat and Dreft and Marmite just like them.'

'But, pet, don't you see — that's just it!'

'What's just what?'

'Shopping like that *isn't* normal and respectable for a single young man. It's unnatural for someone like you to live alone. By these people's standards it simply isn't done.'

Mafeking Gardens showed it didn't think me fit to cope soon after I moved in to Miss Williams' cottage. Mrs Beesley from No. 17 (Hillcrest) came to my door and offered to come in and do for me twice a week. I said thank you very much but I'd manage all right, and by thanking her profusely I got her to go away in not too much of a huff. But I saw her stop on the way home to tell Mrs Robson at No. 15 (Croft View) all about it, and I saw her shrug her shoulders in my direction . . .

'Did you know we were walking out, pet?' asked Jane as she pushed open my garden gate.

'We're *what*?' I leant my bike against the wall and let us in. 'Is that the same as going steady?'

'That's it, darling — what every Riddleford boy does with every Riddleford girl.'

'The way of a man with a maid. . . . Signifying matrimony?'

Jane laughed as she hung her coat on a peg. 'Oh no, I don't think you're committed to anything. But take care if you walk out with someone quite different tomorrow. You'll have to bear with all the cats of the neighbourhood shaking their heads at your flightiness. . . . What's for supper?'

'No idea — look in the larder and see. . . . Do the neighbours talk about us, then? How did you hear all this?'

Jane rummaged among the cans and mostly empty jars on my shelves. 'Actually it was Shelagh who told me today at the tea-shop. You know that old biddy who comes in every day — the painter one who comes up to Riddleford every summer and paints those dreadful pictures of The Birthplace and flogs them to the Americans and has a gay winter in Florence on the takings? Well, she came up to Shelagh and started talking about "Jane's young man that she's walking out with". All most serious. Shelagh almost died telling me.'

'I think it sounds rather sweet, like something out of Hardy — Pair of Blue Eyes and all that.'

'Can you really make a meal out of spaghetti and canned apricots and tomato juice and onions and a scrape of Stilton?'

'I don't see why not. Didn't they teach you *anything* useful at that college of yours? . . . Was Shelagh's old biddy disapproving?'

'What, of us walking out? I don't think so. What's it to do with her, anyway?'

'Most people don't wait to be asked to pass moral judgments on their fellows — especially in the country.'

Jane had a frying pan hissing on the gas. 'You'd think folk would be more tolerant in the country.'

I asked why and she said, 'Think of all that goes on in country novels — Mary Webb and *Cold Comfort Farm* and so on. Rape and seduction on every page. Wicked Squires and Millers' Daughters — rustic life is well-known to be bursting with sex. All those animals having babies all over the place — it's bound to affect people.'

'If they're so keen on sex,' I suggested, 'they should be crazy for Grimsby's poems. Enough sex there all right.'

'Perhaps they have so much already in their lives, they don't need to read about it.'

'Could be. Anyway, we'll know what the people of Riddleford think about Grimsby next Thursday when the *Courant* comes out. That ought to shake 'em up a bit.'

'Not a hope, pet. They're just a lot of sponges, that's what they are. They don't mind soaking in whatever comes their way: but when it comes to giving in return . . .' She left the sentence unfinished and made a rude face instead. 'Supper's ready, such as it is.'

XII

IF THE WORLD IS GETTING YOU DOWN
TREAT YOURSELF TO A RIDDLEFORD BROWN

it said on Brandon's tumbler-ringed beermat. Brandon set down his pint of bitter on it, folded his *Courant*, and exclaimed, 'Wow, has your Mr Grasmere taken his vorpal pen in hand!'

'You think he's been trenchant enough?' I asked.

'Magnificently trenchant. Never I ween have the gentle readers of Riddledale known such trenchancy. Mark my words, Geoffrey Marston, this is a red-letter day in the history of the *Riddleford Courant*.'

'I'd like to think you were right,' I replied. My write-up had been nicely placed on the front page, with blurred photos taken by Godfrey of the Colonel, Mrs Bunting, Joe Higgs and the Rector, and equally blurred versions of what I vaguely remembered them saying about Lemuel Nightly.

A World Fit for Grimsby

On an inside page, beneath the heading *From The Editor's Window*, was Mr Grasmere's own piece:

It ill behoves the citizens of this our town to be vaingloriously proud of our heritage, albeit to have begotten so illustrious a son as Nicolas Grimsby is no mean honour. We have ever sought to share that honour with the rest of mankind: we have welcomed with open hearts the countless pilgrims who come to visit the spot where the bard was born and where he passed so many of his days.

Nor has the *Courant* ever been a foe to honest inquiry. Minds which seek the truth without fear or favour have never failed to find a friend in these columns. But when the sour note of envy is heard behind a specious display of disinterested scholarship, it is time to lay aside our forbearance. It is time to sound the clarion of alarm!

Such an occasion is at hand, friends.

Heaven forbid that we should accuse Dr Nightly of envy. Our fear is rather lest others take his words and twist them to their own infamous purposes.

We are plain, simple folk. Not easily moved, but, being moved, not easily persuaded to sit down beneath our smarts. To any whose ambitious minds may lead to seek to wrest our favourite son from our arms, we say Beware. For you will find the citizens of this town more zealous to guard their treasured rights than the tigress to protect her young.

A year ago I would have been amazed by Mr Grasmere's exalted tone. But by now I had learnt that in the *Courant* everything has to be pitched a few notes too high if you want to make it heard.

Even as it was, for the greater part my editor's fighting words were sure to be spent on empty air. Riddleford would read what he had to say. It would nod its head and agree that something should be done. And then it would turn the pages to more important matters — to where its name actually appeared in print as the runner-up in the Ladies' Open Golf Championship: to where there's a picture of young Alice Sims from down the street that got married Saturday to young Jimmy Paterson, and what a nice couple they make. Or to the cricket match against Hexham Wednesday which would surely — oh, certainly — have been an overwhelming victory if there was anything like justice in this world, if the Hexham umpire had been anything but deaf and dumb and blind, a moron, drunk and incapable, and almost certainly bribed into the bargain.

The citizens of Riddleford are not, let's face it, an excitable crowd. The great events of history will pass them by without stirring more than a momentary curiosity. Here, if anywhere, the end of the world will be met with equanimity, and Judgment Day be treated as familiarly as a Harvest Festival.

I suggested some of this to Brandon, and gave my opinion that my editor was wasting his time.

'Well, but even so it's good that someone should speak up. Whether you approve or whether you don't, these people's great-grandfathers built up Riddleford's tourist trade: it'd be a shame if today's generation should sit back and let anyone who pleases walk off with their property.'

'But what if Nicolas *doesn't* belong here? Suppose this man Nightly is *right?*'

'You know, Geoff, I hardly think that matters so very much. Whatever anyone proves or disproves, Riddleford has made Nicolas Grimsby its own.'

XIII

O Riddleford Banks, where once I wont to tread,
By Melancholy's pointing finger led,
And wandered in the early Flush of Dawn
Where Riddle's waters blush to greet the Morn.
Twas there, methinks, some Water-Nymph inspir'd
My Infant Muse, and oft with her conspir'd
To sing the Praise of thy translucent Spate,
And all thy several Beauties to relate!

So, in his charming *Delights of Misanthropy*, composed in 1757, sang Ezekiah Hopkins. I quote it because he, better than any other, can claim to be the first Grimsby tourist.

You can picture him leaving his rococo Blackheath home, with its grotto and its Gothick gazebo, and setting his sensitive face towards the north. You can picture the sensation he made as he descended, stuffed to the top-knot of his powdered wig with sensibility, among the barbarous bumpkins of Northumberland. Leaving his chaise, and fortifying himself with a pinch of rare perique, he leans his sentimental breast against the wall of Saint Bridget's Church-yard, gazes at Grimsby's tomb, and muses misanthropically on The Mutability of All Created Things, The Transience of Fame and The Compensations of Philosophick Retire-ment — perhaps repeating to himself those lines of Nicolas himself,

> *The Prize of Fame is but a fayre Deceipt:*
> *All is meer Dust, and Durt beneath our Feet.*

After which he choked back his griefs for the evening and returned to The Grimsby Head — even in those days the best-reputed hostelry in Riddleford — to tuck into a meal lavish enough to keep a poor scholar of the 1960's fed for a week.

The good citizens of Riddleford do not realise how much they owe to Ezekiah — how the essays he wrote when he got home were the starter's gun for the procession of pil-grims which has never ceased to our day. Were it not for Ezekiah's rhapsodies to his friends in the coffee-houses, our town might never have been able to cash in on the accident that brought Nicolas into the world a stone's throw from the parish pump.

XIV

ACCIDENT: I use the word advisedly.

For accident is clearly the word to describe the poet's first appearance in this world. It seems certain that nobody — neither his father nor his mother nor his mother's husband — was particularly pleased to learn of his impending arrival.

There are as many theories about Grimsby's ancestry as he has biographers. Perhaps the best guess is that which makes him the illegitimate son of the Baron Otterburn, whose country seat at Gooseleigh stands to this day just a few miles outside Riddleford. As for the mother, she is usually taken to be a Riddleford girl, daughter of a merchant of the town. Anyone who knows Riddleford girls will find this suggestion easy to accept. Pretty they may not be, nor intelligent nor witty nor especially clean. But nobody has ever complained that the girls of Riddleford are uncooperative.

Did Nicolas attend the Riddleford Grammar School? The Headmaster will show you a mark scratched on one of the school benches:

N.G. his Marke MDCXXVIII

The date is about right if you take it — as most do — that Nicolas was born around 1617. If you believe in those scratches, you will probably also swallow the legend which tells how the boy first attracted attention when he was caught poaching salmon on the Gooseleigh estate. Any resemblance between this story and other legends you may have read is, of course, pure coincidence.

Haled before the Baron — the formidable Cranbourn Goose, he who may or may not have been the boy's father — the young lad so delighted the great man by his ready wit that he was at once shanghaied into the baronial service. In these stories anyone haled before great men invariably succeeds in delighting them with their ready wit: either there was a great deal more ready wit about then, or barons were more easily amused.

If the boy were really the baron's by-blow, no legend is needed to explain how Nicolas got himself into the red and yellow livery of the Gooses, and wended up to London proudly bearing their motto 'Quy Oie Voict Trouvera Aygle'. By the age of twenty Nicolas was in service at the court of Charles the First and — again legend runs true to pattern — turning all hearts by his winning ways and boyish good looks. Before the Civil War he was sent on one or two diplomatic missions to the Low Countries: when war came he was wise enough to side with what appeared to be the wrong party, and spent most of the Commonwealth interregnum sharing the royal exile in the most fashionable cities of the continent.

At the less strictly moralled courts of Europe Nicolas seems to have lived the Good Life and lived it hard: and now he first began to make some reputation as a poet. He had already had a bunch of madrigals in Hardhand's *Galaxie of Gladsome Gems*, but there is little in these innocent catches to foreshadow the greatness to come. Now, during his exile, his poetry takes on more of its characteristically erotic cast: this is the period of what many consider his finest verses, which even today cannot be found outside distressingly limited and formidably expensive editions: this is the period of *Loue's Furniture*, of the unique *Remonstraunce to his too Ardent Mistress* and that incomparable sequel to Ovid's *Ars Amandi* whose 'lewdnesse, licentiousnesse and lecherousnesse' nearly earned the reckless poet banishment from the by no means squeamish court of Naples.

With the Restoration Nicolas too returned to his native shores, hoping for a pleasant sinecure after so many years of loyalty. Alas, none was given him — not even after he wrote his long meandering *Nulla Fidem*, that strangely uncharacteristic poem, so pure that it is set regularly for school examinations with only a few dozen stanzas requiring expurgation. Perhaps, indeed, the very tediousness of the poem persuaded Charles not to reward the poet: for the five thousand lines, as generations of schoolchildren have learnt to their cost, contain no sentiments more original than that one should never put one's faith in princes and that one should retain spiritual resources to bolster one up against the disappointments of this Earthly Pilgrimage. . . .

Frustrated of his ambitions, Nicolas retired to Riddleford and devoted himself to his Muse. Those who find that the earlier poems, though brilliantly outspoken, are nevertheless somewhat superficial in their scope, are wont to prefer the productions of this later period. Certainly none will dispute the eminence of that splendid comedy, *Virtue at Hazard*, said to have shocked even the young Earl of Rochester: nor *The Faithless Friend*, a perhaps somewhat melodramatic but refreshingly frank tragedy of incest and rape in Renaissance Venice.

The biographers frequently compare this period of Nicolas Grimsby's life with the solitary retirement of a hermit. Saintsbury speaks of 'The Sunset Period', others refer to 'the Autumn of his days'. His poem *The Vayle* is often quoted:

> *Vainlie, Content, I sought*
> *To compasse thee at Courte.*
> *But now in this Delightfull Spot*
> *I find thee where I sought thee not.*

But it seems clear that the poet's life differed from the hermit's in several significant respects. For one, he certainly showed no sign of abandoning the favourite pursuits of his exile. Bubbles' Anez Guck was but one of many. There is of course the famous — if almost certainly apocryphal — legend which links his name with that of Lady Jane Goose: a romance on which as many female novels have been based as the Unhappy Loves of Mary Queen of Scots. It was not long before Grimsby became a leading figure in the district. With the exception of a number of law-suits regarding the paternity of certain children, he seems to have been generally popular; and those same law-suits earned him respect as well as popularity with all but the fathers or husbands concerned.

Venerated and esteemed, he died in the fullness of time at the close of a contented and well-filled life. As to the cause of death, the only evidence is the curt mention in Aubrey's *Brief Lives*:

A World Fit for Grimsby

'. . . a surfeit of botteled Ale, and a
fayre comeley Wench named Alisoun.'

He died in 1671, aged 54 or so. And you can dig his bones
if you're so minded in Saint Bridget's Churchyard.

XV

NOBODY knows for certain when Nicolas was born.
They don't even really know the year, let alone the
month and the week and the day.

This kind of confusion is what scholars love most. Into
such mazes they scurry in droves — some with slide-rule
and compass, others with faith and rule of thumb: some with
bees in their bonnet, others with axes to grind. In this
instance they have found references in his poems cryptic
enough to be twisted into any shape you like. As he
himself says:

> *Some Treasoun in the Skyes,*
> *Some Mischiefe high aboue the Earth,*
> *Gouern'd my Birth*
> *And fixt my dolefull Destinies.*

In those days the date of a man's birth mattered a good
deal, for it enabled you to judge a man's character pretty

soundly if you knew his astrological set-up. At the start of supper you tactfully led the conversation to a discussion of the Equinoxes, from which it was an easy step to the state of the celestial bodies when your guest was born. You were a pretty average numbskull if by the dessert course you had not learned whether he could safely be left alone with the family silver or your youngest daughter.

Arguing from similar astrological data, many scholars had attempted to fix precisely Grimsby's birthday. By the turn of the century the context had narrowed itself to two finalists — someone unpronounceable from Uppsala and someone unspeakable from Durham. Each proved his case beyond all possible refutation, with ample evidence and incontrovertible reference. The Swede had written in English, the Englishman had written in Esperanto, and both were translated into every language this side of Sanskrit. There seemed to be no way to reach a decision.

'As if it mattered,' you might say. But it mattered a great deal to the people of Riddleford. For they, looking for a convenient peg on which to hang even bigger and better tourist attractions, had decided that a whopping great festival could be built round the excuse of Grimsby's Birthday. If only they knew when it was. The Englishman thought it was on January 27. The Swede made it May 5.

The people of Riddleford did not hesitate. Gallantly they cast aside all narrow chauvinism, all petty considerations of national pride. The Swede was right, they declared. Of course he was right. How could he be anything else but right — how could Nicolas possibly have been born at a time of year when the streets might be thick with slush and the Riddle covered with ice, when the excursionists would want to stay at home and the icecream sales be negligible?

So Riddleford plonked for May. Ever since when, Herr Wotsit of Uppsala has enjoyed a somewhat exaggerated repute as chronologist, while poor old So-and-so of Durham never quite made the grade. But that's academic life.

From that day to this, Grimsby's Birthday has been piously celebrated, a little more splendidly each Season, until today it is the reddest of red-letter days in the Riddleford calendar. Everyone has a holiday — bank managers and schoolchildren and greengrocers and plumbers: everyone except policemen and lavatory attendants and waitresses like Jane.

It is Riddleford's wildest wonderfullest day in the whole wide wonderful year.

XVI

BRANDON gatecrashed on me early in the morning while I was still in bed. When I opened my eyes I saw that May the Fifth had broken bright and clear. Jim our space-seller tells me it always does: it may rain for Carlisle Races, he says, or the fair on Newcastle Town Moor, for the Riddledale Agricultural Show or the Hexham Fête: but never for Grimsby's Birthday.

Bright and clear it broke — but not *too* clear ('Sunne before breakfast, twill rain at last' — OLD SAW): a nice reassuring haze hung over Riddleford ('Morning haze — Perfect days' — another OLD SAW) which would certainly lift towards noon and leave a stinkingly hot day behind it.

I threw on some clothes and lurched into the living-room. When I opened the window in came gulps of preheated air. 'Going to be hot,' I remarked.

'You can say that again.'

'Coffee?'

'I already put it on for us.' Brandon knows how to make himself at home.

So we sat and ate toast and honey and drank coffee and smoked our first Gauloises of the day on my front step, and watched Riddleford getting ready for The Day.

We could feel in the air that this was going to be something special in the way of days. We could hear people not making the ordinary day-to-day noises. We could hear the husbands not going to work, the kids not running to school. Instead, mums bustled about past the upstairs windows of Mafeking Gardens: the girl from Ferndene came out to empty something in the rubbish bin, wearing an apron over her smartest frock, the one she usually wore only when she went demurely out with her young man on Sunday afternoon.

'Nice piece,' Brandon observed.

I said I hadn't noticed.

Brandon said, 'Ah'. Then he said, 'I brought Nightly's book back, by the way.'

I asked what he'd thought of it.

'Light reading for the masses. . . . Well, if it amuses people, good luck to 'em, say I! The trouble is, you can prove anything if you've a mind to. I once read an utterly convincing essay showing that Napoleon was a solar myth.'

'But you're not convinced by Dr Nightly?'

'Not me. But I'd hate to have to convince anyone back again who was convinced that Nightly was right, if you see what I mean.'

In Mafeking Gardens the children came out to play in their starchy best. Normally scruffy urchins had their hair watered down, while their sisters sparkled with fluorescent ankle-sox and pink plastic butterfly hair-slides. Their mums were zipped into their frilliest and floweriest — the cut-a-dash dresses they put on only for Women's Institute trips and outings to the seaside, up to the neck and down to the knees in hollyhocks, poppies and roses.

Just before ten their menfolk began to appear. A late lie-in with the papers and a second cup of tea had given a good start to the day: now they in their turn were smarmed up for Grimsby. White silk neckcloths impeccably folded under the jacket collar, brightly gleaming boots, on the hair an extra dollop of Brylcreem and on the Brylcreem the best cloth cap at a jaunty angle. Out of the houses of Mafeking Gardens we watched them come, hands in pockets and whippets at their heels, one waiting for another at the front gate, whistling with tolerant impatience: and finally, just as Saint Bridget was striking ten, walking purposefully off towards the public houses.

'How about a drink?' suggested Brandon.

'Good idea.' I scrambled into a few more clothes, buzzed the Remington lightly over my chin, and came out to join

Brandon in the sun. The day seemed hotter already. We walked gaily into town, sharing the town's feeling of expectation.

'They're fond enough of Nicolas today, at any rate,' I remarked.

'You bet — they'd be fond of anyone who gave them the excuse to keep the pubs open all day long by special licence!'

As we neared Market Square, 'There's old Sid sitting outside The Grimsby Head,' I remarked. 'Trust him to be there from the word go, the old phoney!'

'I don't know, Geoff — maybe he's better that way than if he were the genuine article.'

'How d'you make that out?'

'It's so much more English. . . . After all, you must admit he'd be insufferable if he *were* the genuine article?'

'I'd say he was insufferable as he is.'

Riddleford puts up with Sid Grimsby only because *someone* has to be the Oldest Inhabitant — the visitors like it. And it's Sid's right, nobody denies that. But it's a pity they couldn't find someone who would play the part with a better grace. There he sits outside The Grimsby Head, drinking all the beer he is offered — but making no secret of the fact that he would rather have a Pimm's or at any rate a Dry Martini. His behaviour over the pewter tankard is characteristic, too. Some well-meaning Canadian presented The Grimsby Head with this tankard for Sid's own particular use: but the old blighter swears he'd sooner drink from a jerry.

Nor is he any more agreeable when it comes to conversation. Every now and then some programme like *Tonight*, short of material, sends someone up to ask him to what he attributes his many years. They are lucky if they don't get the dregs of Sid's beer in their face. They will ask the same dam-fool question, every one of them: and Sid always flies off the handle, asks the young fellow what he means talking about 'many years' like that, and let him wait till he's Sid's age and then see how pleased he is when some cheeky nipper ups and asks him how did he get to be that ancient?

The other question they all ask is about his name. You would think that, sharing the same name as the town hero, Sid would try to make something of it. He's had the chance often enough. Sam Hartpool, Chairman of our Council, has tried many a time to talk Sid into it. Said he'd see the Council made it well worth his while. But the old man stuck his heels in and wasn't having any. 'Poets!' he said in a voice of infinite contempt. 'They hasn't been no poets in my family yet, thank God, and they ain't going to start to be none now!'

But a poor show is better than none, and so Sid goes on. He throws his weight about disgracefully in Meg's — Lady Margaret's Hospital, that is, Lady Margaret Goose having bestowed it on the Parish of Saint Bridget two hundred years ago for the housing of five old men and five old women. Sid lords it there, being the oldest: and there is nothing the other nine can do but hope their turn will come.

So Sid still sits, scowling at kindly strangers but drinking their drinks, steadfastly refusing to curse modern inventions and they scientists — for, as if all his other irritating perversities were not enough, Sid holds that modern times are better far than when he was a youngster. He adores the television programmes: he cranes his neck to follow every passing jet: he visits the Plaza three nights a week and sits in the front row eating popcorn and icecream and commenting loudly on the action of the film.

'Mornin', Sid,' exclaimed Brandon as we passed the old man, using what he fondly imagines is the local accent. 'Hot enough for you? Not a patch on what it was when you were a boy, I dare say!'

'Balls,' replied the Oldest Inhabitant, rising beautifully to Brandon's bait. 'We never 'ad weather the like of this in my young days. Best Birthday I ever seen, this 'un is. Never seen a one like this, that I hasn't.'

He lugged a horrible red handkerchief out of his pocket to mop his face with. After that he drained his already empty glass and set it noisily down in front of him. Just in case the point had been lost he picked it up and peered into it as if to examine something of interest, then set it down noisily again on the table before him.

He made his point, but we pretended we hadn't noticed and left it to be refilled by some more gullible stranger. He scowled at us as we waved cheerily at him and passed on our way to The Fox & Chicks.

XVII

THE Fox & Chicks was already pretty full. Riddleford's menfolk were very wisely making careful preparation for the day to come. The more one got on board now, while things were fairly quiet, the better.

Brandon and I carried our drinks outside into the Square and watched everything going on.

The Square was baked in sunlight. The shadows were like holes in the ground. The only disturbance which moved the flags hanging from every window was the hot air convecting off the sunbaked paving stones. There were plenty of sightseers about already, behaving as if by buying their railway tickets to Riddleford they had bought a share in the town and intended to get their money's worth — strutting and swaggering in the pride of their temporary possession.

Contrariwise every now and again we saw on the face of some native of Riddleford a dazed look — as if *he* were the stranger and it was really the visitors who owned the town. Other citizens went about with the assured look of family retainers who know their place and are content to minister to others — dispensing Nicolas in small helpings while keeping the keys of the cellar firmly in their own keeping.

Cars swept into the Square, tried to park, and were told they couldn't by wearily polite policemen who got more weary and less polite as time went by. So off they drove again where the policeman said, to the emergency car parks. Cyclists were pouring into the town like brittle locusts, and you could see the trail of their passing, for everywhere they went they shed their chromium-bright machines, leaning against walls while their masters strawed up cokes in snackbars.

From the direction of the railway station poured thick streams of sightseers, squirted out in brief spurts as trainload after trainload hit town. Most of them, too, headed straight for café, pub or coffee-bar.

Over and above the hooting of the cars and all the other
sounds, the playing of the Band in the Public Gardens came
to us fitfully through the shimmering air. We heard them
end the Light Cavalry Overture with a crescendo of relief
and relax gratefully into the Minuet from *Berenice*.

Dogs lay flopped on doorsteps. Cats walked dispiritedly
along walls and the dogs just looked up at them, grunted,
and laid their heads back along their paws, flapping their
tails just once. The cats sat down and started licking themselves and closed their eyes and fell asleep instead.

Only the children seemed as if they didn't know it was a
hot day, but rushed around with their usual appalling
energy, looking at all there was to see and shouting to one
another about it, scribbling on scraps of paper the numbers
of the exciting foreign cars which came in slowly with the
tide, and in the intervals whizzing off to Mars in their
rocket-ships or mowing down the odd horde of blood-
hungry Apaches with the plastic Prairie Pistols they'd won
from their puffed wheat packets. They shot me dead and I
died and they shot Brandon and he died but when they
went across to old Sid Grimsby and shot him dead he didn't
die so they had to go and find someone else.

Small boys were already clambering for good perches
on the American Statue. Any other day this would have
been desecration and a constable would have chivvied them
off double quick, but today the police had too many other
things on their minds. So the boys climbed right to the very
top, resting their feet on the baby's upturned face to get a
foothold to the summit, parking their ray-guns on Nicolas'
mother's bosom and squatting on the splendid grandstand
of her head.

'You writing this all up for the *Courant?*' Brandon asked.

'No — Alec's the Ace Newshound today. His shorthand's twice the speed of mine so they give him all the big speeches.'

We decided we wouldn't even try to get a proper lunch. By now Riddleford was distinctly bulging, and the scrum inside every café would be shocking. I thought sympathetically of poor Jane while Brandon and I ate our sausage rolls and cheese and drank more beer at The Fox & Chicks. By this time the beer was warm and not very interesting. After that we went across to the Town Hall to watch the Distinguished Visitors arrive.

Sam Hartpool was already there with his old woman, of course, and all the other members of the Urban District Council and their wives. Colonel Jonson-Platt. Mrs Bunting — but not Harold Bunting, who was avoiding the ceremony as he avoided all his wife's social observances. Mr Grasmere from the *Courant*, ex officio. The Rector and Mrs Dwindle. Professor Bissentine and a pair of colleagues from the Foundation, in their thick hot robes, looking more than usually sheepish.

The Municipal Officials were there in force, dressed in smart suits and looking as though they could be depended on to do a sound job of work. The Town Crier stood apart in his dazzling uniform: Riddleford hadn't had a town crier for centuries, but just before the war they decided to revive the office in the interests of the tourist trade. He had a simply splendid uniform and very little work to do: but today was his Big Day and he looked anxious. He also looked a little thirsty, but then who didn't?

Mr Egerton Smythe, Conservative M.P. for Riddledale, drove up in a large and important-looking car. An even larger and more important-looking car brought Lord and Lady Otterburn from Gooseleigh. The Lord Mayors of Newcastle and Carlisle arrived, and the Vice-Chancellors of half-a-dozen universities, all in their robes — the lesser-known the university, the gaudier the robes. Then there were the Headmasters of some of the Northern public schools, with the Headmaster of Riddleford Grammar School trying to be on equal terms with them. The Bishop and his good lady bowed graciously to Mr Dwindle.

And then a shoal of foreigners — the crowd saying Ooooooh about some and Aaaaaah about others. The Africans in their fancy native dress were the ones everyone loved best: the dull Commonwealth representatives in their natty pin-stripes we found rather uninspiring.

Finally, preceded by a long murmuration of anticipation which you could hear rippling down the street, came a bigger-than-ever car, bearing the Guest of Honour, General Douglas Gruenberg of the U.S. Army, hero of the Second World War ('What did he do, for Chrissake?' whispered Brandon, and I said well, if he didn't know I didn't see why I should be expected to, except wasn't he the one that always carried a hand grenade tucked in his webbing, and Brandon said no, I was muddling my *Sunday Times* serials) — General Gruenberg, now President of Erie University and several million Americans' favourite for the next Republican President next time the United States needed one.

Amid a spatter of uninformed applause the General left his car, looked happily round at us all, gave a friendly wave and walked up the steps and into the Town Hall. Press cameras flickered like summer lightning — I noticed Godfrey among the photographers — as the General paused in the doorway for a final wave. Then the doors were closed, and two red-faced policemen stationed themselves outside them, their hands behind their backs and their legs apart, taking no notice of the catcalls — 'Don't let 'em out, Charlie boy!' — thrown at them by the ruder elements among the crowd.

People started to disperse again. It would be a long wait before the Distinguished Visitors reappeared, for even without the speeches the Ceremonial Lunch was bound to last a couple of hours. Some of the sightseers stayed firmly where they were to keep good places for watching the start of the Procession — sitting down on the pavement and drawing Thermoses and sandwiches out of their plastic shopping bags. I saw Phoebe Stuart-Stotts and some of the rest from the Foundation making a picnic on the pavement right outside David Greig's — a rather liquid picnic it looked, too, by the number of cans of beer passed foaming from hand to hand. Others wandered away in search of better positions or some more amusing diversion: they attached themselves one by one to one of the scores of queues — the queues for lunch, the queues for icecream, the queues for hot dogs, the queues — longest and slowest of all — for the Ladies.

XVIII

Aʟʟ over Riddleford lay a mellow attentiveness, as though, in recognition of the unlikely heat, the town were taking a siesta, but keeping one ear cocked in case anything exciting crept up on it unawares.

Traffic had ceased in the centre of the town, the hooting and the shouting died away. The excitement of the crowds, which at first had been a boisterous Blackpool enthusiasm, settled into a passive acceptance. For the next few hours they would take whatever was dished out to them, now in the official section of the day. Only later would they be thrown back on their own initiative and be forced to find their own entertainment.

There was a certain amount of mysterious activity round the Town Hall when important people with important expressions hurried in and out past the policemen. Every now and then a false alarm would set the pavement-squatters Oooohing and Aaaahing prematurely. Towards three o'clock more police woke up and started to clear the Pro-cessional route. The crowd was eased back and split like the Red Sea by Moses till a clear strip of roadway appeared, empty but for the Chief Inspector and his saluting minions who came hurrying up to him to be given fresh orders and hurried away again to carry them out. The tension grew.

And it didn't seem to be any sort of an anti-climax when the great doors of the Town Hall were flung open and the

Distinguished Visitors appeared — looking taken aback by the sudden glare of the sunlight and the wild applause which greeted them. They smiled self-consciously into the newsreel cameras.

'They look as if it was a good lunch,' said Brandon. 'But they're not looking forward to their afternoon walk, I'll bet!'

I don't suppose they were. But there was no avoiding it — the Procession is the most sacred of all the rites of the Birthday. Without the Procession the Birthday might be just any old celebration: it's the Procession that sets it apart: it was the Procession that all these people had come all this way to see. It contained almost everyone who could be squeezed in on any pretext whatsoever—

— the Boy Scouts and the Girl Guides and the Wolf Cubs and the Brownies and the Boys' Brigade, all with flags and banners.

— the Fire Brigade, highly polished and clanging, and the nurses from the hospital (well and truly wolf-whistled at) and a section from the nearby R.A.F. station looking pink and serious, and a detachment, very slick, of the Riddleford Territorials, sweltering in their thick uniforms.

— the boys of the Grammar School accompanied by their Masters. The girls of the Grammar School — more whistles — with their Mistresses.

— the Salvation Army (with band) and some cadets (with fifes) and the Girls' Training Corps (with Northumbrian Pipes) and the Choir of Saint Bridget's shepherded by two beaming curates in billowing surplices.

76

— the huntsmen (mounted) of the Moorland Riddle foxhounds.

— a farmcart filled with petrified infants from the Primary School depicting 'The Spirit of Riddleford' with an assortment of highly symbolic objects.

— the cast of the Grimsby Players in their costumes for *The Faithless Friend.*

— this year's Queen of the May (prettily blushing) and her Moss Trooper, and last year's Queen of the May and *her* Moss Trooper, accompanied by sundry outriders, pages and other camp-followers.

— Miss Smethwick of the girls' Grammar School on horseback as Lady Margaret Goose, the one who founded Meg's — a delicate tribute to Lord Otterburn.

— the Churchwardens from Saint Bridget's and the representatives of the Women's Institute and the Young Farmers with their prize-winning goat and the British Legion and — I really can't imagine why — the Lord's Day Appreciation Association.

— and all the foreign visitors talking among themselves in foreign languages.

— and all the Distinguished Visitors, a triumphant, tired finale.

The Processional route is a long way from being the shortest line between two points. No right-minded crow would fly anywhere near it. On a day like today, with the ceremonial Luncheon settling most unceremoniously within, the Important and Distinguished must have felt that for once the Unimportant and Undistinguished had the laugh on them.

After forming up in some sort of order outside the Town Hall, they set off up the High Street, fifes and pipes tooting and wailing magnificently while the players were still un-blown. A left turn up Grimsby Street brought them to The Birthplace. Today is no day for airing your heretical doubts about whether The Birthplace is genuine or not: as the Procession passes the old building, heads are bared and silence falls. The Fire Brigade hold their bell and even the trumpets of the Salvation Army are hushed. A simple solemnity, but nothing could more profoundly impress our transatlantic visitors. Nothing is heard but the shuffling of feet and the whirr of ciné-cameras. The Americans are pastmasters of processional, but the majesty of silence is an ingredient they have overlooked.

Applause erupts all the fiercer after The Birthplace. A short cut takes the Procession through narrow, cobbled Scholar's Alley and alongside the spiked railings of the Grammar School. Then back into the High Street and across the traffic lights which someone has forgotten to switch off so that they are flashing their instructions at nobody, pathetic and Casabiancan. And so, hot and dusty, weary and perspiring, the Procession enters Market Square.

Like many others, Brandon and I had cut across from the Town Hall to Market Square. Knowing the terrain better than most we found ourselves a vantage-point which gave us a Vistavision of all we wanted to see. More and more spectators swarmed after us into the square till it was jammed solid with a muttering, murmuring mob.

The Procession did what it could to make itself comfort-able, and settled back to have speeches made at it. The flags flapped limply overhead: the crowd trembled with anticipation. The Town Crier stepped forward into a gale of cat-calls which he only just succeeded in weathering. He cleared his throat impressively — timidly, in fact, but the amplifiers made it impressive — begged silence if we pleased, and called upon the Honourable Member of Parliament for the Division of Riddledale, Mr Egerton Smythe.

They don't have beauty contests in the House of Commons — more's the pity, maybe — but if they did I would back Egerton every time. Slim, elegant, debonair — all that a *Woman's Own* hero should be — he's a smasher on the telly and right in his element on an occasion like this.

In honour of the day he was in his 'City' rig. Mr Smythe has two basic uniforms. There is his country one, tweedy and coarse, tricked out with such accessories as a rough-hewn pipe, fox's head tie-clip and even — rumour has it — occasionally a deftly placed wisp of straw. These he wears in the House or for big London meetings: together with a faint whiff of the local dialect, they suggest to his colleagues that he is reluctantly sparing them a few hours between getting in the barley, tilthing the silage or gelding the roan stallion.

Needless to say he wouldn't dare pull that one on his own constituents. They know him too well. On his own ground Egerton is the City Man: one of themselves always, but at the same time a fellow that knows his way around, who'll stand no nonsense, who can handle those government bastards up at London.

He began his speech today with an apt quote from Grimsby:

Why singes my Muse of foreyne Climes,
Of antick Deeds and antick Times?
Lo here lo here our Sunne best gleames
And baths us in his brightest Beames!

The recitation was hailed with enthusiastic applause from the perspiring crowd. 'What's so wonderful about that?' Brandon wanted to know. 'Struck me as pretty corny.'

So I explained about Egerton Smythe. It had all begun with his maiden speech, when — hard to imagine — he had been a nervous beginner. I don't know what it was he was trying to push, but whatever it was he backed up his argument with an apt citation from Grimsby — neatly turned enough to earn a flicker of applause from older men who saw he needed encouragement.

It says something for Smythe that there and then he saw he had a potential gimmick to his hand. The feeblest of quips passes for wit in the Commons: this was more than that. Ever since then, Egerton Smythe has never delivered a speech without a quotation from Nicolas — it has become his trade mark, even if it is only to ram home a small point arising from the Opposition's objection to the Board of Trade's minute respecting the price-restrictions retrospectively operative on the re-import and consequent re-sale of (synthetic) parrot food.

Coyly modest and shyly smiling, Mr Smythe waited for the applause to fade. Then he proceeded diplomatically to butter up the influential citizens — whether Conservative, Liberal or worse. Gradually his scope widened to include more and more of the electorate until almost every one of the sweating, baking, jostling crowd felt he had been individually singled out for compliment.

It was a lovely lovely speech, the molassy waves lapping in one ear and out the other, telling us how here, now, on this auspicious occasion, the hearts and thoughts of all true lovers of England were turned towards Riddleford; and the citizens of this town, born in liberty and nursed in the rustic freedom of the green countryside, might permit themselves a flush of pardonable pride as they reflected how, over the arches of the centuries, men of all colours and creeds, in all manner of walks of life, had turned to a son of Riddleford as the purest, most lyrical champion of all that was fairest in our heritage, all that was closest to the hearts of right-thinking men the world over, wherever men were free to respect the legacy of the ages, not bound to serve the fettering whims of a synthetic ideology. . . .'

'I wish to flipping hell he'd get a flipping move on and let the pubs open again. That's the only flipping freedom I'm concerned with!'

And as if Mr Smythe had heard the remark of the man standing by us, his speech spiralled to a standstill like a helicopter coming to earth. Mr Egerton Smythe knows better than to be a bore. He sat down amid tumultuous applause and wearily passed a careless hand through his unruffled hair.

The Town Crier waddled forward again. He called upon General Douglas Gruenberg to speak to the people of Riddleford. The crowd, about one-thousandth part of which consisted of the people of Riddleford, stirred slightly more awake, roused by the thrill of hearing in the pink flesh the hero the newsreels had so often shown them blurred and pale and grey . . .

General Gruenberg stood, coyly pretending to be embarrassed by the warmth of his reception. 'Next to of course God America I . . .' Brandon quoted, but that was not the General's line.

First he told us, with a soldierly grin which we could see even from the far end of Market Square, that he supposed he was a man to whom the pen was less familiar, we might say, than the sword. Nevertheless he was convinced the pen *was* mightier than the sword and he would tell us why. Back at the Pentagon — what we would call our War Office — in Washington, he had learnt through long experience that if he wanted anything done it was no use his trying to do it himself. No, instead he asked his secretary. It made him a little thoughtful to think that a girl of — well, no, he wouldn't tell us her age, we knew how women were about these things, but that a girl that young should get things done where an old campaigner was helpless! If that was not proof that the pen — nowadays perhaps he should sooner say the typewriter — was mightier than the sword, then he'd like to know what was!

He was the more privileged to be here on this auspicious occasion, he went on, when we might have thought that a man of arms would consort ill with these men of letters: and, indeed, he did feel a little *hors de combat* — which didn't, by the way, mean what he'd always taken it to mean, war-horse, *hors de combat*, war-horse, but he understood from a friend who spoke *français* that it meant something quite different. But he thought he could claim some right to be here on this auspicious occasion, addressing this fine British crowd, because he too had been a lover of Nicolas Grimsby and all that Nicolas Grimsby stood for, and it was a love he

guessed he never picked up at school, whether his attention
was always wandering or his teachers just didn't bother, but
during the period of his courtship, the girl who was later
to do him the honour of consenting to become his wife had
always used to sit out on the back porch of an evening and
read poems to him — Grimsby's poems — and so there had
been bred in him a love of those verses which the passing
years had never effaced, so that as an instance all throughout
the last war in Europe he had always carried the Pocket-
book edition of those poems in his baggage and when he
took out this book in the thick of the fiercest fighting it
would bring him a comfort and a new belief he might go
so far as to say in the western democratic way of life itself:
and he felt then, and he felt today, that the poems of Nicolas
Grimsby were a link between the free peoples of the world
— a solid bond which the storms of war and the tempests
of catastrophe only made more binding — stronger than
any mere geographical tie because it was forged and made
fast in the hearts of the people.

And so on. And if the amplifiers took hold of the poor
man's articulation and threw the words away without
anyone being able to catch hold of them, what did it matter?
We all knew he was saying nice comfortable things to us,
wasn't he?

At last he sat down, and mopped his brow amid boisterous
cheers. The Town Crier called on the Chairman of the
Urban District Council, Councillor Samuel Hartpool.

Sam, who had been dabbing at his face with his hankie for
some time, hastily stuffed it into his official sleeve and
struggled to his feet. Shouts of 'Who's minding the shop?'
and 'Where'd you park the plough, Sam?' — the Coun-

cillor's everyday business was managing an agricultural machinery repair shop — all witnessed to that ready wit which is one of the most attractive features, is it not, of the English character, today just as in Nicolas' day.

Sam opened his mouth. 'My Lords'n Ladies, Ladies'n Genmen. We're gathered here today on this auspicious occasion to celebrate . . .'

He got that far. And then he received, neatly on the side of his red face, a very well-selected and well-aimed tomato.

There was a moment's terrible silence.

The red juice trickled delicately down his cheek. It dribbled meticulously on to his clean white collar. You could see why it's always tomatoes they choose.

The crowd, which for a moment had paused on the brink in a splendid hush, broke into a seething murmur: and then instantly hushed again as a shout rang out:

GRIMSBY FOR GRIMWICK!

And behind the shout, louder and firmer, echo on echo, came more and more shouts from more and more voices: GRIMSBY FOR GRIMWICK, GRIMSBY FOR GRIMWICK, GRIMSBY FOR GRIMWICK!

XIX

WE couldn't at first see who was doing what, or even where. The whole crowd was peering into itself everywhere. Shrieks and shouts rose from all sides, but it was like in caves, you couldn't tell where they really came from.

'There they are — look, over there!' Brandon's voice showed that he was trembling with excitement. He seized my arm in a biting grasp and pointed.

Sure enough, over in the corner of the Square, on the steps of the Plaza Cinema, a section of the crowd looked even more confused than the rest — a little maelstrom whirled faster among the heaving waves of heads. Dust flew up into the air to confuse the issue yet further, but we could see that people were waving things. Big white placards had been pushed up above head level, whose slogans we could just make out as they twisted and jolted in the hands of their bearers:

GRIMSBY FOR GRIMWICK!

DON'T BE RIDICULOUS —
GIVE US OUR NICOLAS!

GRIMWICK WANTS JUSTICE — AND GRIMSBY!

RIDDLEFORD'S SHAME —
GRIMWICK'S GLORY —
GRIMSBY!

'Let's go take a look,' suggested Brandon, and we started moving towards the disturbance. Quite a number of other people seemed to have the same idea: quite a lot of others seemed to have quite the contrary intention: so it was all rather Lars-Porsenaish, those behind crying Forward and those in front crying Back.

Two or three policemen were moving forward, rather hesitantly, not quite sure whether it was students or drunks or communists they had to deal with. Children were crying, girls were shrieking, strong-voiced men were saying strong-voiced things.

'Whoever can it be?' whimpered a shopgirl close by. 'Whoever it is, let's go get 'em!' said a tough-sweatered farmworker, elbowing his way towards whatever it was.

Over on the rostrum I could see poor old Sam Hartpool looking most embarrassed, wiping his neck, obviously trying to make light of the matter before his Distinguished Guests. The General was leaning forward with a professional interest, and even Mr Smythe was looking a little less disdainful, as if the afternoon were proving just a spot less of a bore than he had anticipated.

We were nearing the centre of the disturbance by now and matters had become a little clearer. 'Look,' someone shouted, 'that man there's Billy Robson!'

A roar rose from the crowd.

'Who's Billy Robson?' Brandon wanted to know.

'Fast bowler of the Grimwick cricket team,' I explained. 'They hate his guts here — claim he doesn't play fair.'

'You mean that little guy there using his placard as a weapon?'

'That's the fellow. If they get him they'll have the bollocks off him!'

A voice nearby shouted 'Come on, lads, let's skin 'em alive!' and a number of Riddleford men, who had been leaning against walls waiting for the speeches to be over with and the pubs to re-open, looked at one another, nodded without a word, buttoned their jackets, rubbed their wrists, and started to barge their way purposefully to the attack. They had looked forward to today, but they'd never dared hope they'd get a real good fight laid on as part of the official entertainment. Normally, if there was to be any fighting they would have to provide it themselves, outside pub doors at closing time. This was far better, with the enemy none of their friends, drunk or larking, but those traditional foes, the men of Grimwick.

The fighting was spreading. The men with the placards were following Billy Robson's lead and using them as clubs, cracking them down on their assailants' heads. The police weren't here in any numbers yet, and two or three groups of men were slamming it out hard enough, encouraged by the bystanders. Reinforcements were arriving for both sides: yells and shrieks filled the Square.

Then 'Uh huh, here they come now!' exclaimed Brandon. 'Now for it!' The police were moving in — a dozen or so, shoving their way firmly through the crowd and easing the onlookers back. The fighting broke up as they drew near: the Grimwick men, hopelessly outnumbered, dropped their placards and took to their heels, disappearing into the crowd where there was little chance of capture, not with so many other strangers here. The newsreel boys reluctantly swung their cameras back to face the rostrum again, and the ceremony was ready to continue, its dignity only a little impaired.

Sam Hartpool had wiped most of the tomato from his face and stepped forward again, searching for the thread of his discourse. But fortunately the disturbance had been bad for his memory. He fumbled about for a moment or two, then suddenly brought his carefully rehearsed speech to an abrupt close by thanking us all most profusely — quite what for, I wasn't very clear.

Vast applause from a grateful crowd, who had been settling down to another flood of talk but were delighted to be excused it. We were hotter than ever after standing in this press all this time: above all things we wanted the ceremony to be over and the pubs to be re-opened. There was a sigh of relief that swept from one end of the Square to the other when Sam bowed to Lady Otterburn and invited her to lay her bouquet.

The Floral Rite is the true climax of the Birthday Celebrations — 'this moving ritual, symbol of our devotion to the ever-blooming genius of our poet' as Mr Dwindle has described it. The idea is that every virgin in Riddleford should lay a bunch of flowers against the American Statue as a tribute. It's a lovely, lovely ceremony: the Americans adore it.

The term 'virgins' is not too rigorously applied. Any unmarried girl may take part, for, as Brandon points out, with girls as precocious as Riddleford's, there wouldn't be much of a showing if the Authorities got technical.

Tradition demands that the first bouquet be thrown by Lady Otterburn, the county's First Lady. 'Does she have to be a virgin too?' Brandon wanted to know. Up tripped a fat little girl in pink frills from the Eliza Dobson Ecole de Dance who simpered and thrust an enormous bunch of frothy pink flowers into Lady Otterburn's arms.

Amid deafening cheers the first bouquet was laid. Lady Otterburn then stood back hastily to avoid being trampled to death by the wild horde of stampeding girls who now tore forward with *their* bunches. In no time at all the statue was almost lost from sight beneath a blanket of flowers.

And it was only when the tide receded — when the troop of girls had all deposited their offerings and returned to their mothers — that it was seen. . . .

Someone — and it could only have been one of the girls — had produced from somewhere yet another placard. And there she had stuck it up among the bunches and bouquets, under the very noses of the crowd: there it leant against the base of the Statue, stark and defiant:

NICOLAS GRIMSBY—
THE GRIMWICK POET

XX

THE scrum for the pubs started the instant the speechifying was over. I don't know what the foreign visitors must have thought, watching the English dive for drink. They must have got the impression that

Riddleford men are all confirmed alcoholics, living a per-
petually lost weekend, unable to last three hours without
refuelling.

On our way to The Fox & Chicks we passed Alec, very
excited, with Godfrey the photographer, his camera at the
ready.

'How's it going?' I called out.

Alec waved a well-filled notebook at me but dashed on
without a word. 'Got some lovely shots of the scrap in
Market Square,' raved Godfrey. 'Real documentary stuff!'
They went on their way.

'Godfrey certainly got a break,' I said. 'Nice change from
prize sheep and silver weddings.'

'Scoop of the year for the *Courant*,' said Brandon. 'Don't
you wish you'd been on duty?'

Everyone, needless to say, was talking about the incidents.
By now the police had cleared away the offending placard
from in front of the statue, and perhaps the local C.I.D.
were testing it for fingerprints, and maybe questioning
the several hundred virgins who might have done the
deed.

'Maybe it was no virgin,' Brandon suggested. 'Maybe it
was a secret agent from Grimwick, *disguised* as a virgin!'

'It will look well in the *News of the World* — "Accused
yesterday of masquerading as a virgin, Albert Simmons, 48,
of The Laurels, Grimwick, pleaded Guilty and asked for
fifty-seven similar offences to be taken into account".'

'You would think the other girls would have noticed if
one of them was carrying a ruddy great placard instead of a
bunch of forget-me-nots,' I added.

'Must've been rolled and hidden — hidden I don't quite

know where, though. There was a girl at school parked her gum in the elastic of her knickers. Would there be room for a placard, I wonder?'

'How should I know?'

'Well, in any case a secret service virgin would be sure to know a simple thing like how to carry a placard in her undies. And of course there was a hell of a rush, and they'd all be so excited about throwing their own bouquet. . . . You know what, Geoff, I expect Riddleford is thick with Grimwick agents. All these crowds — who knows who they are really? I doubt if they're normal visitors, any of them. I think the entire population of Grimwick is here, pretending to be visitors. They held up the true visitors early this morning as they passed through Grimwick in their cars or trains. The real ones are still over there, thousands on thousands of them, trussed up in the streets and leant against walls, while the dogs walk from one to another sniffing at them. And the inhabitants of Grimwick have whipped their cameras and sandwiches and come here in their place.'

'But why?'

'Aha, that'll reveal itself later. What we've seen so far is just Phase One of the Master Plan. So far it's been jolly fun, but this evening it won't be fun at all. Grimwick will be battling for her ancient rights — the red fires of revolution have been smouldering for years and now they will break out into ruddy flame. Blood will flow tonight in the gutters of Riddleford. The firelit sky over Riddledale will astonish the burghers of Carlisle. And from every lamp-post will hang bodies — starting with the Urban District Councillors.'

'What can we do to be saved?' I exclaimed. 'We must rescue Jane while there's yet time!'

'She can fight alongside us, like Russian guerillas. She was a Girl Guide, wasn't she? It's to them Riddleford must look for her safety! Ein feste Burg our Guides are still!'

So we finished off our drinks and set off rather hysterically towards The Clay & Wattle. It was about time Bill and Shelagh let Jane off anyway.

XXI

'Y OU'VE been drinking!' Jane, a bit red about the gills and her hair flopping distraughtly over her forehead, was indignant.

'Get a move on then and catch up!' I replied. Jane said she'd be with us in two ticks and vanished to powder her nose. We sat down at a half-vacant table by a suspicious couple who drew their plate of cakes to their side of the table as though they thought we might steal them. Shelagh brought us coffee.

Then Jane reappeared, looking considerably refreshed, like in those strip ads where the woman is just about dead in the first frame, and then in the next — five seconds after taking a WHIZVITE tablet — she's had a new hairdo, changed into a revealing low-cut party frock with a soundly engineered bra beneath, had some plastic surgery done to her profile, and lost ten years of her age. Our suspicious couple took one look at her and — not recognising the person who had served them a short while before — stretched an arm to protect their sugar too.

'Well, did Nicolas have a happy birthday, you lucky people who saw everything? Nice speeches, nice procession, nice everything?'

'Well, you heard what happened?'

'No — what happened? Something exciting? Some of the customers who came in earlier on seemed excited about something, but I didn't know it was anything special. Was it?'

'Only war's been declared, that's all,' remarked Brandon airily.

'War? What are you talking about? Who's declared war on who?'

'Grimwick has. On Riddleford.'

'Oh, don't be so maddening, Brandon. Geoff, tell me what he's talking about before I lose my temper.'

So I told her all about everything.

'Golly, d'you think it's serious?' she asked after it all.

Brandon laughed. 'You remind me of the Duke in *The Faithless Friend*, when he asks Malfacio:

> *Are these the Maskers who are come to swelle*
> *Our sport with their droll Fancies?*

and Malfacio answers . . .'

> 'No, my Lord,' Jane interrupted eagerly,
> 'I fear they are in Earnest! — isn't that right?'

93

'What's this I hear — people actually quoting Grimsby
asked a new voice. 'I thought we'd done with him no
that the speeches are over.'

'Don't be so bloody cynical, Harold — come an
join us.'

Somehow room was made for him in our corner, an
Harold Bunting brought his cup of coffee into our mids
He gave a grunting sigh. 'The truth is, I *am* feeling a litt
cynical this evening.'

'I know what you mean,' I said.

Harold sighed again and relapsed into silence. Silence i
Harold's habitual state — he seems to sleepwalk through lif
as if it was part of a dream he's dreaming, like a man wh
was once taken by W. B. Yeats on a day-trip to Fairylan
and has never quite got over it.

If Hilda Bunting always has her feet firmly on the ground
her husband's are always a little off the surface of the earth
The only time he gets anywhere near to grips with th
world we live in is when it is something to do with hi
painting. His parents christened him Harold Caravaggic
Bunting hoping that by sympathetic magic his name woul
help him to greatness, and he has been trying to live up to i
ever since.

Sheer persistence, and a wide range of experiment, can'
help but get one *somewhere*. If you skip through the back
numbers of the art papers you will find Harold's name
cropping up quite often, if seldom in the boldest type-
sizes. What success he has enjoyed has been, paradoxically,
because he has never hit upon a personal idiom. Chopping
and changing over the years, by sheer mathematical
inevitability — the monkeys on typewriters writing Shake-

speare trick — he has found himself every now and then not a straggler but a leader in the van.

When this happens, the critics, for whom normally he is a source of embarrassment, leap at him and tell him They Always Knew He Had It In Him. They predicted this promise back in 1933, didn't they? He becomes temporarily the rage, and in espresso bars from Camden Town to the King's Road you will hear his plastic values and tonal texture analysed and admired, while Bright Young Things still in their first tartan trews and pony tails offer to swop all the modal refinement of a Robin Ray for one fifth of Bunting's sense of timing.

When thus for a brief moment the limelight catches him, it does not affect Harold in the least. He still mooches about contentedly obscure, toying with new theories, wondering whether perhaps he might paint better under the influence of mescalin, or whether the discipline of Zen might be some help. . . .

'Well,' Jane declared, '*I* don't intend to be cynical tonight. I intend to enjoy myself.'

'Harold will think you're fiddling while Riddleford burns,' said Brandon.

Harold smiled his slow smile. She asked him if he thought the afternoon's outburst was meant to be taken seriously.

'Not the outburst itself, no, I don't think so, Jane. That was just pranking. But you don't find an eruption like that without something seismic beneath.'

'So you think Grimwick *is* serious about it?' Brandon nodded. 'Judging by everyone here, Riddleford doesn't seem especially worried.'

We all looked round at the other inhabitants of the tea-shop — a little fewer now, as the visitors started to leave for home or else devoted themselves to evening pursuits. The prevailing mood was one of apathy. The couple at our table looked back at us aggressively: whether they were eavesdropping or not, they were certainly hostile. Perhaps they came from Grimwick.

'On days like today,' said Jane, 'Riddleford makes me rather sick. Grimsby is just something they sell over the counter, carved up into souvenirs and busts and gift editions. I think it would serve them jolly well right if Grimwick *did* take this Nightly theory seriously.'

'You're being a little unfair, aren't you?' Brandon objected. 'I don't think you can expect Riddleford to go on being crazy about Nicolas twenty-four hours a day. It's like marriage. The first fine careless rapture gets worn into something more practical for everyday use.'

'At least husbands and wives don't usually ignore each other completely: which is what Riddleford does to Nicolas.'

'Well, yes: but think how tired you'd get with all these tourists poking their noses everywhere, telling you how lucky you are to be living heah, heah in the vehery heheart of England, where sang the sweheetest caroller of them ahall. . . .'

Jane pouted. 'I suppose you're right in a way, but it still seems ungrateful.'

'If Dr Nightly's book does have any effect,' I suggested, 'it might shake people up.'

'Cheerful Charlie!' said Brandon. 'But in any case I think you're wrong. I didn't notice riots and indignation meetings after your old Grasmere's effort. It was just as you yourself said it would be — response nil!'

'Hilda was talking about this book,' Harold put in. 'Would you say he's made out any sort of a case? Has he a leg to stand on?'

'Quite a nice leg, if you ask me,' Brandon answered. 'He seems to have some quite formidable guns on his side.'

'Should go down well in Grimwick!'

Harold laughed. 'I dare say the Grimwick Public Libraries ordered three dozen copies on the day of publication. Think how it must have taken the fancy of the Mayor and Corporation!'

I asked how he meant?

'Well, just imagine if you were the Mayor of Grimwick. Ruling a dirty old city without a single thing to attract visitors — except a few mills that might just stir some dour Dane studying Industrial Conditions. And that ugly old Saxon cross they have in the Strawmarket, carved all over with phallic symbols which the guidebook naïvely refers to as "an unusual floral design". But not a thing else. And from your window in the Town Hall you see the cars and coaches streaming past on their way to Riddleford, shaking the plaster off your walls and the tiles off your roofs: you hear the hoot of the trains on their way to Riddleford, you hear the tinkle of the cyclists' bells — and not one of them stopping to put a single penny in the pockets of Grimwick tradesmen. . . .

'But what if Dr Nightly could prove his case!

'Why, then you'd see people buying goods from *your* stores and filling their cars with petrol at *your* garages and

eating meals at *your* restaurants. They'd buy postcards of
Grimwick, peppermint rock with GRIMWICK all the way
through, busts of Grimsby made by Grimwick craftsmen
in Grimwick factories and sold in Grimwick shops by Grimwick girls. The trippers would suck Grimwick ices and
lick Grimwick candy floss and visit Grimwick cinemas when
it rained: they'd park their cars in Grimwick car-parks and
spend their pennies in Grimwick loos: and finally they'd
settle their bills at Grimwick hotels and drive away from
Grimwick with their pockets empty but the back of the car
filled with Presents From Grimwick!'

'Stop, Harold!' Brandon cried. 'You should be a writer,
not a painter! You make me want to rush out and dynamite
The Birthplace right now, just to bring a little holiday to the
Mayor of Grimwick's heart.'

'Perhaps he's already planning to do it himself,' said
Jane. 'After today, who knows what he may be up
to?'

'I don't think things have quite reached that stage yet,' I
said. 'It's only a book, after all.'

'Don't forget what General Gruenberg said,' Brandon
reminded us. 'The typewriter is mightier than the
sword.'

'Yes,' Jane added, 'and as Harold says, it's just what
Grimwick wants to hear. . . . Well, if they're so keen to
have him, and if Riddleford couldn't care less, jolly good
luck to them says I.'

'Jane — blasphemy!' Brandon exclaimed. 'Even in jest
you shouldn't say such things!'

She turned to Harold Bunting. 'What do you say?'

'Oh, I'm not so cynical as you. . . . Have you ever looked

at Grimwick? Properly, I mean? You should get Geoff to take you there on your next afternoon off and take a good look round. . . . Most industrial cities manage to get parts of their heads above the soot and the grime: they develop a sort of rugged rocky character of their own. But not Grimwick. Grimwick's just a rubbish-tip dumped into Riddledale, like those heaps of tin cans and old prams you suddenly come across right out in the country where nobody seems to be living for miles. . . . You know the Riddle as it passes through Riddleford — sparkling, clear? Well, it's the same river that flows through Grimwick, but you'd never know it. It is murky, smelly, hurrying between the bleak black walls — hurrying to leave the town as fast as it can. But it can't hurry fast enough. It can't escape the dirty old men who lean over the parapet of that Iron Bridge they're so proud of and spit their tobacco-juice into the water. It can't escape the Elementary schoolchildren with their icecream cartons and toffee wrappers which float on its surface like the Lady of Shallott only stickier. . . . And finally, just as it's perhaps thinking to itself that it's reaching open country once more, it has to run the gauntlet of the gasworks . . . that gasworks! Filling the Riddle all day long with sludge and slag and silt and heaven knows what other dreadful things, not even good enough to be made into gas!'

The two strangers at our table had sat watching Harold during this declamation with a look of furious disgust. As he finished, they scraped their chairs back, placed three pennies under a saucer, and left us ostentatiously. 'Definitely from Grimwick!' whispered Jane as they paid their bill and left.

'Proving my point!' said Harold. 'I don't want to be a dog in the manger, but I don't think I could stand having Grimsby go *there*!'

XXII

WE sat in silence for a while, meditating.

Then Brandon said 'Well, shall we be moving on?' We got to our feet, said goodbye to Bill and Shelagh, and emerged into the open.

Outside, the evening had settled on Riddleford — the warm May evening, heavy after the sunshine, busy with midges, drowsy and exciting at the same time. After the animation of the day, natives and visitors alike were sinking into a contented lassitude.

'Well, what's everyone planning to do?' Brandon asked.

'Somebody said something about fireworks,' Jane prompted.

'Yes, that's right,' said Harold. 'Fireworks down by the river. But they'll be later, when it gets properly dark. Before that there's a concert — Northumbrian songs, *Blow the Wind Southerly* and *Blaydon Races* and Eightsome Reels and that sort of thing.'

His suggestion was received with polite silence. Then Jane voiced all our feelings: 'I don't think I feel quite up to folk-song tonight. I know one *ought* — but somehow I feel in the mood for something cheap and vulgar. . . .'

'Aha. Then that rules that out. Then I believe there are some stalls down by the Riddle — shooting at things and throwing things at plates and fishing for things: that more your line?'

'That sounds better. Will there be anything to eat? I've just remembered I'm starving — I've been too busy feeding other people to eat a mouthful all day.'

'Oh yes — there'll be plenty to eat — I don't know about cheap but certainly vulgar. Toffee-apples and candy-floss and jellied eels and cockles. . . .'

'Just what I need!' Jane exclaimed.

So we all set off together towards the river. As we neared the Recreation Ground we could see there was quite a lot going on. Not just stalls but a Roundabout and Dodgems and a Whirligig which looked very frightening. A blast of indiscriminate noise came out to meet us, and we could see crowds of saunterers whose faces were pink, blue and yellow from the Chinese lanterns.

We parked ourselves in front of a flaring naphtha-lit booth, eating Bert's Unbeatable Bullburgers washed down with some firewater named Hapi-Kola. The wheezy sound of worn-out pop-songs came from the Bumper Cars. On the sign for Bert's Bullburgers some wag had rubbed out the 'b' of 'Unbeatable', achieving a closer approximation to the truth: the Hapi-Kola tasted even more like aerated cough-mixture than most of its kind: but it didn't seem to matter very much. The tawdry food, the coarsely amplified rock-'n-roll, a fierce tourney in the hurly-burly of the Dodgems — if it wasn't much of a way to show our respect for Nicolas, at least it seemed wiser to forget him for the moment than to fret over his doubtful future. We could fret tomorrow: tonight it seemed wiser to explode our feelings skywards with the rockets than to pickle them inside us with mild-and-bitter, glooming on a pub-bench moping mum.

XXIII

FUN and games. But while Riddleford and its visitors were enjoying the sound of revelry by night, others must have been burning the midnight electricity. In particular, it must have been just at this time that Dr Nightly was working on his interesting postscript to *A New Evaluation*.

News that a second portrait of Nicolas Grimsby had been found was a thrill for scholars and antiquarians the world over. His lifetime was one when almost everyone, whatever his rank or title, got himself immortalised by a painter in the course of his life: a man as eminent as Nicolas would certainly have been portrayed time and time again. Yet the only certain portrait of him we have is the Robsart Portrait — the one you know and I know and everyone knows, the one that's in all the books. It was painted by Thornaby Robsart, Painter-In-Ordinary to the Household of Charles the Second, in his later and even slicker manner. Once it was in the possession of the Gooses. Then Lord Otterburn — to save on the insurance, rumour said — presented it to the people of Riddleford, who hung it in The Birthplace.

If you look hard and show willing you can see it's a portrait of *somebody*: but only a brave man would commit himself further than that. On the back some seventeenth-century handwriting declares the masterpiece to be ye Authentick Representacioun of Maistre Grimsbie as he was in his Lyfetyme seuerall tymes seene by me Josiah Humble — but who Josiah Humble was, and why it was thought necessary for him to write this testimony on the back of the painting, is uncertain.

Out of the gloom that passes for background in Stuart paintings there peers a face. Not, frankly, much of a face: you would need to be in a very friend-of-humanity frame of mind to interpret its expression as anything but utter inanity. Was this, truly and honestly, the face behind which lurked the mind that drove the hand that penned the lines which have stirred our hearts all these centuries? Rather let us believe that Nicolas had it painted expressly for some Coy Mistress whose coyness he was not particularly anxious to overcome. However, it is worth something running into six or seven figures — a price that would provoke respect even in a Greek shipowner.

And now, a few weeks after the Birthday Celebrations, a new portrait of Grimsby was presented to the world.

The romantic story of its discovery was described in Dr Nightly's addition to his earlier book. Grimwick Town Hall houses a collection of full-length portraits of past Mayors, and these, it seemed, were in the process of being cleaned when one of them was found to be painted over another and earlier work. Nobody was much interested in the subject of the overlying painting — he had done nothing remarkable and had been dead over a hundred years anyway

— so over the protests of his descendants his likeness was removed, and London experts were summoned to examine the portrait thus revealed.

Seventeenth century, all were agreed.

Genuine as could be.

Very interesting, they muttered, very interesting indeed.

Artistically there was little for the critics to be excited by.

But in the top right-hand corner there was an inscription:

Nic. Gri. Mai 5 MDCLXII aet. 45

1662? Yes, Grimsby would have been just about 45 then. And May 5 was his birthday (according to the Uppsala theory, at least) which seemed more than mere coincidence.

A comparison between the face of this portrait and the face of the Robsart painting was not very revealing, though this is not very surprising. Much more significant is the background of the picture. For here we have, not the customary murky gloom, but a naturalistic landscape. Or townscape, rather, for the subject is depicted as standing with an air of proprietorship outside a large and accurately drawn building: and the building is one which can be identified, for it stands in an old street in Grimwick!

XXIV

YOUNG Alec had skilfully managed to describe the Birthday Celebrations for the *Courant* with only the mistiest of references to the vulgar demonstrations. Now the paper met Dr Nightly's new discovery with the same polite scepticism. In private, Mr Grasmere admitted that it looked like a nasty smack in the eye: but he told me that he had no intention of yielding an inch in public until the matter was proved for certain. So for the present the *Courant* put a bold face on things.

The Editor of the *Grimwick Clarion*, on the other hand, had a good deal to say. No matters were minced in its caustic columns, no bushes were beat about. The placard incident, declared the *Clarion*, was the writing on the wall which it ill behoved the complacent citizens of Riddleford to ignore. The Editor thought he could hardly do better than remind us of the words of Nicolas himself:

> *No Man liues so vnto his fellowes, but*
> *he is his own strictest Master; nor is*
> *so subiect to the Legislacioun of others,*
> *but his sternest Iudge is still himselfe.*

In accordance with this principle, said the *Clarion*, the people of Riddleford should consider the new evidence dispassionately and judge the case fairly.

The *Grimwick Clarion* was not alone in finding the Birthday episode and the new discovery newsworthy. The National Press had also pounced — the dignified papers with dignified regret, the vulgar papers with vulgar glee.

CRISIS IN GRIMSBY'S TOWN

wrote one newspaper, adding:

BUT WHICH IS GRIMSBY'S TOWN?

Another paper wanted to know

ANYONE ELSE WANT THIS POET?

— a considerable testimony to the importance of the event, for in the normal course of things this paper never mentioned poets and artists: to qualify for admission, they had to have interesting divorces or gas themselves in Chelsea ovens or sell their works for enormous sums in cash.

RIDDLE OF RIDDLEFORD

was the headline from Printing House Square, while more sensational papers described the situation in our town with commendable imagination:

Today, in the normally bustling streets of this quaint old market town, the air is tense with disquiet. Everywhere, on street corners, in shops, by the quiet of their own firesides, the townspeople of Riddleford are gathering and uneasily asking themselves this one anxious question: <u>Have they any longer the right to claim Grimsby for their own?</u>

The entire community is overwhelmed with the shadow of tragedy darkening the sky. Overnight, from a peaceful rustic township, Riddleford has become a hotbed of doubt and suspicion. Its citizens confer in furtive whispers. Neighbours eye one another with distrust . . .

The picture that we, on the spot, saw was slightly less dramatic. The good people of Riddleford were not noticeably asking themselves any questions at all. A few old ladies might sigh, delighted, how shocking the whole thing was; but Dr Nightly's proposition seemed too absurd to merit any serious discussion. If the topic was raised in pub or barbershop it was soon abandoned in favour of matters of greater moment — the weather, cricket, taxation.

Even Mr Grasmere saw in private no need to take too grave a view of things, for all his declared trenchancy in public. He came into our office to talk to us all one morning. Seating himself unsteadily on Alec's City Desk, he discussed what should be the *Courant's* attitude.

'On the whole, I think we should count ourselves grateful to this Dr Nightly. One rather welcomes these disturbances that the scholars kick up from time to time. They rouse public attention — and that's always a tonic for circulation.'

'If you look at the dailies, sir,' Alec objected, 'you'll find that public opinion's a lot of it against Riddleford.'

'I don't think one need worry about that, Alec. I hardly think there is any serious danger of this professor proving his case, do you? When you have lived in this town as long as I have, you will know better than to start taking the scholars seriously. . . . Excuse us, Geoff: no offence meant.'

I laughed and said none taken. But I added that I didn't see how a controversy could do Riddleford any good.

Jim, our space-seller, who was paying one of his rare visits to his office, interrupted. 'Ah, you're wrong there — isn't he, Mr Grasmere? Riddleford's like a film star — same line of business, you might say. And it's with Riddleford like it is with a film star — scandal does nothing but good. Divorces, motor accidents, getting boozed up at parties and taking their clothes off — what would make the neighbours shake their heads and call the police if it was you or me, man, it's meat and drink to them actors. Packs the people into the cinemas, if you know the star takes drugs or beats his wife or goes to naked parties. Well, Riddleford's just the same.'

'Jim's perfectly right,' Mr Grasmere agreed. 'Look on it as a tonic, Geoff. That's what this book of Nightly's is — a regular tonic!'

XXV

I F Riddleford had not yet woken up to the serious possibilities of Dr Nightly's proposition, other minds were faster on the draw. The Editor of *The Times* printed a letter that he had received:

A World Fit for Grimsby

Dear Sir — I am no scholar, and perchance would do well to say with the Mantuan, *non nostrum inter vos tantas componere lites*. But in view of the *fracas* currently upsetting one of our Northern counties — a difference which cannot, I take it, be settled by any existing legal procedure — may I presume to offer a suggestion? It occurs to me that an old and tried means of judgment might be revived here to good purpose. I refer, of course, to the decision rendered by King Solomon in a certain celebrated maternity case. One wonders how strong would be the parental feelings of the citizens of Riddleford and Grimwick were it suggested that the Complete Works of Nicolas Grimsby should be divided equally and dispassionately between them?

DUNCAN FORSYTH
Inner Temple

And to 'The Old Dodgers' Column' in another widely read daily wrote another public-spirited citizen:

Alfred Donaghue, of Middlesbrough-on-Tees, writes:

I remember my grandmother, the famous singer Rosie Donaghue, as well-known in her day as Vesta Tilley and many others, once took part in one of Nicolas Grimsby's plays which had been adapted as a musical comedy by the late regretted Frederick Spindle, whom many of your readers may recall as the Resident Conductor of the Pine Court Orchestra in the early days of broadcasting, and your readers may care to know that she never cherished the least doubt that the poet was born neither in

Riddleford nor in Grimwick but in Middlesbrough-on-Tees.

To which the Old Dodgers replied with their customary wit:

> And we have an Aunt in Wigan who is prepared to swear the old buffer came from Wigan! Any offers from Ashby-de-la-Zouch?

Several members of the community received offensive letters from writers who forgot to add their signatures — Sam Hartpool, Colonel Jonson-Platt, several of the staff at the Foundation, and of course the Editor of the *Courant*. 'Nothing out of the ordinary,' Mr Grasmere said to me, 'but they are useful straws in the wind. It's helpful to know on which topics one's readers hold strong opinions.'

He leafed through a handful of papers and showed me a sheet of lined notepaper. 'Here's a typical specimen for you.' I could just make out the childish handwriting:

> Why dont you shut your mout
> you sily basterd what do you
> know about wher Grimby livd id
> lik to now? Grimwick men are
> men and touger then Ridelford
> men ha ha any day of the wek
> and wel bash the day ligts out
> of you durty bugars if you
> dont shut your big mouts.

XXVI

Two days later the phone hauled me out of bed early. It was the office. Gloria said they'd had a call from The Birthplace. Something — she didn't know what — seemed to have happened: could I nip round at once and see? She'd try to get the photographer, Godfrey, out of bed too if she could.

Round I nipped as soon as I could. No shaving, no coffee, no nothing. In a very few minutes I was braking my bike outside The Birthplace. In a town like Riddleford, made up of one-way streets and narrow bottleneck roads that can't be widened because they're lined on either side with architectural gems, the old-fashioned pushbike is by far the most efficient means of transport.

Grimsby's Birthplace is no architectural gem. This is hardly surprising, for great men are not as a rule born great, and their birthplaces have a tendency to be out of scale with their later achievement. But Grimsby's is even less distinguished than most. It is the sort of house a child will draw — a squarish box with two windows up and two windows down, a chimney either end, and not much more: made of stone — cold dark grey stone — and roofed with slate — cold dark grey slate, glinting purple in the wet and streaked with moss.

The Council has done what it can. The walls are whitewashed, creeper climbs over the wall, window-boxes and tubbed plants give it a touch of gaiety which I'm sure it never had during Nicolas's lifetime. But it remains an ugly house, and only eyes misted over with the romance of The Legend can blink the fact.

There was quite a crowd gathered outside when I appeared. A restrained gathering with blank dull faces, gazing vacantly in hope of something happening. A constable here and there held the crowd in place, but the crowd didn't look as if it felt the urge to break through and riot.

Had the Curator been murdered, I wondered? Or had a couple of tourists — honeymooners if we were lucky — chosen this spot with its romantic associations to consummate a suicide pact? Either way it would be something mettling to write up — more inspiring than cattle markets and debates of Young Liberals' Discussion Group's Open Forums. And Mr Grasmere would welcome anything that would boost circulation.

I told the police who I was, and with expressionless formality they passed me in through a side entrance. Flicker of interest from the crowd in case I was a detective from the C.I.D. In the hallway stood the Curator, talking and gesticulating, alive and so far as I could see enjoying his usual health. No razor slashes, no bruises, no blood.

I was disappointed. Not that I had any particular grudge against the Curator, but if someone had to be the victim of an outrage I had as soon it was him as anyone. Doubtless he made a first-class job of purveying Nicolas to the public — far better than Fothergill Jones, for instance, the Official Guide. But Fothergill, though he was a silly ignorant little man, was at least human. The Curator was not. His function of High Priest at this, the most sacred shrine of the Grimsby cult, placed him above humanity. He had never felt, you could be sure, a qualm of doubt about the dogma he retailed. He had remorselessly swallowed The Legend in its entirety, and his strength was as the strength of ten because his faith was pure.

He looked questioningly at me as I stepped into the room, not recognising me at first, obviously wondering why the police had let me through the cordon. I explained myself, and he gave a shamefaced laugh as he said, 'It's just that we don't want the police letting through any pilgrims yet, not till we've cleared this business up.'

'What business?'

The Curator looked round at his companions — a Police Inspector, a couple of men from the Town Hall, and a distressed-looking gentleman in dirty overalls with a handful of cotton waste in his hand. They all looked miserable. 'I suppose there's no harm in letting the Press know?' the Curator asked the Inspector.

The Inspector looked at me and winked. 'If they don't know now they'll know later. They might as well get the story straight.'

So the Curator told me how when he had arrived earlier this morning a shocking sight had met his eyes. In front of The Birthplace, on the lawn, the Friends of Grimsby Association had recently erected a statue of Nicolas. Not an ancient one, of course, but a modern one based on conjecture. Rumour had it that a well-known Academy artist had done it, taking a real classical statue left over from the Crystal Palace, and doing a remodelling job. However acquired, it had been erected with the usual pompous ceremonials and had been ignored ever since, except by the makers and buyers of picture postcards.

Until today. For what had so shocked the eyes of the Curator when he arrived this morning had been the sight of the statue gleaming with a new brightness beneath a bucketful of bright fluorescent pink paint.

And — so that there should be no doubt why the deed had been done — on the very walls of The Birthplace, in the same obtrusive colour, had been brushed the words:

GRIMSBY BELONGS TO GRIMWICK.

'Ah, if only I'd left it at that!' cried the Curator. 'We'd be better off now if I'd done nothing.' But he told me that he had immediately phoned the police and the Town Hall, and the Town Hall had put him through to the Surveyor's Office, and the Surveyor had referred him to the Water Department, and they had passed him on to the Highways Department, and so on and so on. But in the end he had succeeded in getting someone round — the overalled gentleman who was now looking so sorry for himself.

He had arrived prepared to get rid of the paint: enthusiastically prepared, for civic dignity and pride were involved. Perhaps it was this enthusiasm which had caused him to overdo it: or perhaps it would have been the same anyway. Perhaps it was all that anonymous Academy sculptor's fault. But the stuff the Council man produced to remove the paint certainly did a remarkable job. It was a chemical concoction called 'Kleenorl', and the label promised that 'Kleenorl' would remove anything and everything from anywhere and everywhere, effectively and painlessly.

It did, too. Off came the paint in a brace of ticks. Sighs

of relief all round. They'd taught those Grimwick rogues a lesson, they flattered themselves . . .

. . . until it was observed that, like the Sorcerer's Apprentice's broom, 'Kleenorl' was doing its job a little too thoroughly. Bits of stone were dissolving away, morsel by morsel: and though the statue had not completely disintegrated, it had acquired that 'matured' look only found in the busts they dig up at places like Pompeii.

I walked across to the window and admired the finished result. Nicolas now looked remarkably venerable, but less identifiable than ever. Personally I thought the whole incident rather funny, never having been deeply in love with the statue in the first place: but I didn't suppose the Friends of Grimsby would find it amusing, nor the Curator, so I tactfully kept my thoughts quiet for now.

Out on The Birthplace lawn I saw that Godfrey had arrived and was busy photographing the weathered statue from every possible angle. He caught sight of me at the window and waved: a few moments later he came in to join us, twiddling knobs and snapping catches on his cameras as he came.

'Who's the criminal?' he asked breezily. 'A practical joke, is it?'

'Well, it is true,' the Curator admitted, 'we *do* get jokesters — visitors who sign so-called comic names in the Visitors' Book. But never anything like this.'

'Depends, you see,' added the Inspector. 'There's jokes and jokes. Not many would spend a couple of quid on paint just for a lark like that. But some would. So you just don't know.'

'What do you think yourself?' I asked.

'Oho, man, I don't think anything myself. So don't you get quoting me in the *Courant*. But — off the record, now — I have my idea there's more to this than a joke.'

'You think it's meant seriously?' Godfrey asked.

'Well, it's not the first thing that's happened, is it? Mind, I don't say we have any evidence connecting this with any other occurrence which may have occurred, but there's such a thing as a supposition, you know.'

'You're thinking of the Birthday Celebrations?'

'I may be and I may not. But there's that book, isn't there, your Mr Grasmere was on about? Now, if someone was to read that book, and that someone was to start getting ideas . . .'

'So you suspect a conspiracy?'

The Inspector winked again. 'You write in your paper that the police are pursuing investigations, will you? And in return I'll let you know if anything turns up. How's that — is it a bargain, now?'

I said it was a bargain. Then I asked what would happen about the statue.

The Inspector gazed out of the window on to the lawn for a moment. Then — first making sure the Curator wasn't within earshot — he smiled at us and said, 'Don't say anything to his nibs, but I rather like it better the way it is now!'

XXVII

'H e's got a point there,' Godfrey remarked as we walked away from The Birthplace in search of breakfast, me pushing my bike and he sorting out his rolls of film. 'But it'll make a nice story.'

'Who do you think it was?' I asked. 'Grimwick?'

'Well, you can never be absolutely sure, can you? There are always hooligans who hide behind whatever's the current bogey to play the goat, so it might have been them. But I should think Grimwick's more likely. Gang of students, I shouldn't wonder, taking the chance for a lark.'

I said it was going a bit far, doing that sort of damage.

'Don't forget it was our people did the damage. The paint itself didn't do any harm . . . even as it is, I don't know as any harm's been done.'

'No, but it might have been.'

Godfrey laughed tolerantly. 'All right, it *might*. But it *hasn't*. And that's what matters, isn't it?'

Indeed, the Curator seemed to be the only one seriously put out by the outrage. At the Foundation, later in the day, I found that public opinion tended to agree with the Inspector, that the statue's aesthetic appeal had been enhanced rather than otherwise.

The *Courant*, of course, could hardly do otherwise than take a scandalised view of the matter. Mr Grasmere did his usual stuff splendidly, tying up such 'hooligans and hobble-dehoys' with all that was rotten in the world today. But the outside world was for the most part entertained. *Time* magazine, for instance, thought the incident comic rather than tragic. Alongside a portrait of Nicolas captioned:

RIDDLEFORD'S GRIMSBY:
After a tomato, more sauce

appeared these characteristic comments:

Not since critic Ruskin, no word-mincer, accused America's famed mother-limner Whistler of flinging a pot of paint in the public's face, has Britain re-echoed to such an insult. When citizens of Riddleford, tourist-loving birthplace (1617) of risqué rhymester Nicolas Grimsby, woke to find the statue of their favourite son bedaubed with pink paint, there was small doubt where the blame should be laid. Ever since Oxford's forthright Professor Nightly suggested that Riddleford's Grimsby might in fact spring from neighbouring mill-town Grimwick, feelings have run high between the two towns. First blood in this theatrical dispute took the appropriate form of the theater's traditional substitute for gore — tomato juice — flung by unidentified assailants at Riddleford's testy-temperamental Councilor Hartpool. With two clear rounds to Grimwick, tourist agencies are wondering if next season will see a re-routing of their organised pilgrimages.

XXVIII

'WE'VE got to do something!' Jane declared, when we and Brandon met to discuss this latest outrage. Sitting in her cosy bedsitter, we all agreed with her — but what was the something to be?

She poured out more coffee and opened a packet of ginger nuts. We all thought.

'The first question is,' I said, 'are we to retaliate in kind?'

'I don't see that it matters what we do, so long as we keep our end up,' remarked Brandon, sprawled on his back on Jane's divan, gazing up at the flowered wallpaper — Bill and Shelagh had decorated their house with the leftovers from The Clay & Wattle and it looked like it.

Jane, sitting on her legs by the gas fire, munched a biscuit thoughtfully. 'I don't know, you know. All this slopping paint over statues and throwing tomatoes at people — it isn't exactly dignified, is it? I think it would be rather cheap just to give them a taste of their own medicine.'

'But all the same you think we should make a gesture?' I said.

'Yes. Something symbolic, to show we're not going to take it lying down.'

But what was it to be? We drank our coffee and ate our biscuits and looked to one another for suggestions.

'Of course there's one thing we could always do,' Brandon said at last.

'What's that?'

'We could organise our own private boycott of Grim-wick.'

'You mean an economic embargo — we don't do any of our shopping there or anything?'

'That's the sort of thing. If a lot of us got together . . . Not that the loss of our custom will send Grimwick bankrupt exactly, but it's a gesture, a matter of principle, like Jane wants.'

So we agreed on the gesture. We felt very high-minded and virtuous as we allowed ourselves to be governed exclusively, for once, by principle. And we determined to make everyone we knew join us.

But there was a drawback.

Living in Riddleford, you have to be remarkably single-minded to manage without Grimwick altogether. Grimwick has so much that Riddleford, frankly, has not. True, those brochures about Riddleford in your Tourist Agent's dispensers do give the impression that every pleasure man has devised for himself is to be found within a stone's throw of your hotel . . . but when you actually arrive here you may find that life is not such a Technicolor kaleidoscope of delights.

Riddleford does its best. But, naturally, it is thinking first of the tourists, the visitors here for three days from Outer Space, and of the money they bring. And if you're spending only a few days in the town, there's plenty to occupy your time. It's only if you are a more or less permanent resident that the horses on the merry-go-round seem to come round rather too frequently.

Take the Festival, for example.

XXIX

RIDDLEFORD, like everywhere else nowadays, has its Festival. Not one of your splendid Edinburgh-type festivals, with international orchestras and fancy ballet companies and plays in foreign languages. Riddleford's annual Festival of the Arts is much more modest than that.

It offers a taste of everything: and we made the most of it by going to everything we could.

So one evening we went along to the Town Hall to hear the Edelweiss String Ensemble — a group of distressed displaced persons who seemed too unhappy to enjoy even their own music. We could hardly blame them. To spend one's days scratching Haydn divertimenti endlessly in bleak town halls to ignorant audiences, most of whom have come only because the Festival Committee has blackmailed them into buying tickets, and having forked out the money it seems a shame to waste them . . . such a life can hardly help damping the spark that shone so bright when one set off on one's career, when Vienna or Budapest had been so gay, so gay, — when one had all but danced one's way to one's lesson with Herr This or Frau That who had themselves studied under Schumann, no less . . . when one went with a suitor at either hand, one to carry one's instrument, the other to carry one's music . . . and they would wait in the café on the corner during the lesson and run to greet one as one emerged. . . . May-blossom days scented with coffee

from the cafés along the Hofgartensee and lilac fresh from
an April shower and the soft spring sunshine filtering
through the pale lime trees. . . . How could one recall all
that on a rainsoaked foggy one-night stand in Stockton or
Riddleford or Chesterfield, where fat councillors wheeze
and their wives snore during the adagio, where the damp
air curls the pages of the tattered music on the rickety
stands . . . ?

The Riddleford Festival was not intended to show a profit
— not directly, at any rate. If it did, so much the better;
but the prime object was to stimulate trade. So the Committee did not much mind when they lost over the Edelweiss. The prestige was well worth it, and besides, what
they lost on the foreign musicians with their foreign music
they made up easily enough on the English music played
by English musicians.

The Black Hole Colliery Silver Prize Band is none of your
run-of-the-mill pick-up groups. They have actually
performed on the radio, in those embarrassingly hearty
programmes you hear if you switch on too early in
the morning. But it would be unfair to judge them by
that.

It's when they are on their own home ground that you
should hear them: and then you will discover something
that perhaps you never realised before . . . that here is the
true heart of English music. When Albert Pennyman
takes his solo in *The Rosary*, the clear sad sound of his cornet
rising above the gruffer, heavier, larger instruments, you
are getting something that is honestly native, something far
nearer to the Englishman's heart than the sophistications of a
Walton or a Rubbra or even the rollicking gaiety of a

Malcolm Arnold. You are hearing, for once, the English-man's true voice. For this is the only way in which he isn't too shy to reveal his soul. He expresses himself through the Black Hole Colliery Silver Prize Band just as he does when the Salvation Army processes through Grimwick on a Sunday morning when the rain-wet cobbles are glinting in the pale blue sunlight, just as he does when, beneath Sir Adrian's superb baton, the massed bands muster in the Albert Hall.

The Riddleford Festival gives us drama, too. The Grimsby Players are not quite up to the Shakespeare Memorial Company, perhaps, but their hearts are stolidly in the right place. They piously alternate performances of Grimsby's two plays throughout the Season, occasionally diversified with other classics — *The Rivals, Arms & the Man, An Inspector Calls.*

The Arts Council, bless their hearts, provided a travelling exhibition this year — a small collection of modern paint-ings which I imagine they send round to places like Riddle-ford to remind the government that the public does get some return for the money it spends on them. The pictures sit in the lobby of the Town Hall — a hugger-mugger collection of kitchen sinks and grey streetscapes, alongside all kinds of abstracts from the kind that starts with reality but lets it fade out of the picture to the kind that gives it the go-by right from the start. The whole gloomy display was presided over by a desperately arty female from the local School of Arts & Crafts with mauve eyelids and fascinating stockings, who sat at the door and got on with her knitting and was visibly put out when any visitor came in to disturb

her. Not many did, and when they did they were mostly
children on the way home from school, who went round
with wide-staring eyes too awestruck to snicker even.

Somebody tried to talk the managers of our two cinemas
into staging something by way of a Film Festival, but they
weren't having any. With the cinema trade the way it is
these days, they couldn't afford to risk any further decline
in box-office receipts by mounting obscure foreign films
with sub-titles or — worse still — silent classics so scratched
that it seems always to be raining. One manager did go so
far as to offer to put on a Bardot season, but that wasn't
quite what the Festival Committee had in mind. 'It's
Continental, isn't it?' he protested, but they weren't convinced.

The Plaza and the Regal feed us with a twice-weekly
change of programme, but the content is not quite so
variable as this might suggest. The choice really boils down
to two kinds of film. First, Westerns — somebody riding
again, or the kid from somewhere, or the something trail.
Second, romantic melodramas about surgeons who put
medicine before love, soldiers who put the honour of the
regiment before love, women who put careers before love,
executives who put increased production before love — but
who all find, in the end, that Love Conquers All.

Of course there is always the Riddleford Film Society,
which we joined and actually attended now and again. But
it's out of a sense of duty that one goes to their meetings: one comes away sadder and wiser, perhaps, but
one doesn't feel one has had much fun. Documentaries
from the great days of British documentary, all smoking
chimneys and cheerful miners: doctrinaire puppet films

from Eastern Europe with every wooden figure toeing the party line. And — principal attraction of the evening — some inspiring epic of the Bolshevik Revolution, with handsome workers being fearfully decent and capitalist bosses behaving like capitalist bosses. . . . One does not hold hands at this sort of film: one sits forward and is done good to. Which I think explains why we were more or less compelled to visit Grimwick for our entertainment, boycott or no boycott.

XXX

SUNDAY is the deadest day.

That is true of Riddleford just as it is of anywhere else in Britain. There is the *appearance* of life: if anything we have more trippers than on other days. But there is less for them to do. They drift hand in hand looking for something to amuse them, looking with mooncalf faces at shuttered shops, queueing at the nasty plastic-tabled caffs which are always the only ones to open on Sundays, queueing for a boat on the river, queueing for icecream or a cup of tea from the kiosk, queueing for the bus back to wherever they came from and ought never to have left.

This particular Sunday it was raining, too, but it was Jane's afternoon off so we had to do *something*. The Plaza offered Gregory Peck as a cowboy who put cows in front of love only to find that love triumphed in the end. The Regal offered Victor Mature as a gangster with a heart of gold. I forgot what he put in front of love, but I know he was sorry for it later.

'What's on in Grimwick?' asked Jane.

I looked reproachfully at her but she didn't flinch. So I began leafing through the paper. It turned out to be a Double X-citing Attraction, combining *Cat Women of the Unknown Planet* with *The Monster with the Atom Brain*. You couldn't call it a choice at all. We grabbed our coats and hurried to the bus station.

The Lord's Day ends officially at 4.30 so far as Grimwick is concerned, and there is nothing the Lord's Day Appreciation Association can do about it. At 4.30 there was already quite a queue stretching fifty yards from the Palladium doors in the drizzle, four deep and all breathing down one another's necks, dreaming of the warm womb of comfy darkness into which we would soon be usheretted.

Inside, the cinema was boisterous. It seemed to be a rendezvous for the youth of Grimwick: they appeared to be conducting their normal social business despite whatever was happening on the screen, leaning over the backs of their seats or craning past neighbours to swop badinage with friends. And in the double seats, whose very existence showed that the Manager knew why half his audience was here, canoodlers were already canoodling. 'How can they, at five o'clock in the afternoon?' marvelled Jane.

The Palladium seemed a parade-ground for Grimwick's rising generation: the young men were here to show off their prowess, the girls to show off their men, laughing at their wisecracks, encouraging their feats like a publicity agent. Any distraction was exploited to the full — the ice-cream girl was at once surrounded by a bevy of chattering barging youngsters who shut off the screen for some while.

Not that we were in any danger of losing the thread of the film. The girl behind, breathing Spearmint all over us, plotted the action aloud one step in front of the film itself with the same unerring accuracy as a missile-spotting radar screen. As Our Hero burst into the Mad Scientist's secret mountain laboratory just in the nick of time to prevent him flicking the lever which would consign the whole of Los Angeles to destruction, a blasé voice in the row behind commented, 'You'd never guess.'

Close by us were some of the few middle-aged members of the audience — the kind who go every week to the cinema without looking to see what's showing. One old dear we soon wished dead. 'Are you enjoying it?' she asked her companions two minutes after the film began. They grunted. So she asked them what they had said. They said again that, yes, they *were* enjoying it. That satisfied her for a moment. She started looking at the screen again, oblivious to the tumult of the teenagers around her: almost at once she started laughing — really laughing, really enjoying herself she was. 'That was the funniest part so far — didn't you think that was the funniest part so far?' Though what was so funny about those catwomen I don't know unless she was confusing them with Mickey Mouse. When the film finished she was asking 'Did you like it?' before 'THE END' had faded from the screen.

Between the two halves of the double-feature we had an unexpected treat. They showed us a travelogue, about Grimwick. In Gorgeous Kaleidocolor, Breathtaking Bu-Tee-Scope and the full wonder of Horizoscopic Sound.

It was quite something, and it made Grimwick look quite something too. Panning down Corporation Street on a Sunday morning when everyone was at home reading the *Sunday Pictorial* and the streets were like those famous post-cards of Aberdeen on a Flag Day, the cameraman showed us the same building that was in the new Grimsby portrait:

'And here,' the silken religious voice of the commentator purred, 'in the very heart of this lovely old Northumbrian city, is the most cherished of all its treasures . . . the birthplace of the famous poet Nicolas Grimsby. Even today, amid the roar and bustle of modern life, we may fancy that it was along these cobbled streets that the poet must often have wandered — musing, perhaps, on the fame that would one day be his, little guessing that in times to come it would be Grimwick's proudest boast that he was born here and here wrote those deathless lines so dear to the heart of every Englishman. . . .'

It was magnificently done. So magnificently that even we found ourselves on the verge of accepting the commentator's words. He spoke with such *certainty*, he refused to consider that there might be any doubt. . . .

It was still raining when we came out, and the day was just as miserable. We didn't feel any the better for having two X films inside us.

XXXI

WE came away from Grimwick feeling that now the enemy — and by this time 'enemy' was the term we were all using to refer to whoever was behind the Grimsby-for-Grimwick campaign — really had gone too far. This, we felt, was more than we could stand.

But it was what happened the very next morning which finally clinched the matter so far as we were concerned. It might have been planned so that our Sunday night indignation should not have any chance to cool off in the cold clear light of Monday morning.

Brandon had lodgings on the other side of town. His landlady let me into the house soon after breakfast time, when the passages were filled with the sound of vacuum cleaners and Housewives' Choice; she told me I'd find Mr Wayde in bed still.

'Brandon,' I shouted as I barged into his bedroom, 'take a look at this!'

Brandon emerged from his bedclothes, a process resembling a boa-constrictor disgorging its victim. He watched me bleary-eyed as I took his clothes off the carpet and threw them at him. I sat down on the foot of his bed and lit a gauloise and he stretched out for one too.

When we'd lit up, 'Exhibit A,' I said, and handed over a piece of gummed paper, about four inches by two inches, on which was printed:

STOP THE BOTHER AND THE FUSS
GIVE GRIMWICK BACK ITS NICOLAS

and there was Exhibit B—

RIDDLEFORD'S CASE IS REALLY FLIMSY
WALKING OFF WITH GRIMWICK'S GRIMSBY

and Exhibit C—

NO MORE TO RIDDLEFORD NEED YOU ROAM
GRIMWICK TOWN IS GRIMSBY'S HOME

'No wild flights of poetic achievement,' Brandon commented. 'What's the story?'

I told him how the whole of Riddleford was plastered with the stickers. I had found one stuck on the wooden gatepost of the cottage when I left, first thing, and as I passed through the morning streets I had seen dozens more.

At the *Courant* office Jim told me the impudent labels were all over town — on walls and shopfronts and lampposts and notice-boards and pillar-boxes and benches and parked cars and even the blue lamp of the police station. Anywhere where a label would stick. Throughout Riddleford the Council had its men out trying to get them off. I took a look out of Brandon's window. 'Get up and see for yourself.'

Brandon heaved himself out of bed with a groan and tottered barefoot to the window. Drawing back the lace curtain, we could see Jos. Dodds, proprietor of the Family Butchers opposite, out on the sidewalk in person scraping a sticker off his window with a butcher's knife. Farther off, watched by a solemn policeman and two derisive school-boys, a Municipal employee was trying to soak another off a bus-stop. Whether we looked up the street or down, we could see people scratching, scraping, soaking or peeling, some with irritation, others with amusement.

'By the look of it, hordes of them must have spent the night sticking and licking,' Brandon said. 'It'd be easy to find out who did it, just by checking who's short of spit this morning.' He started to tug on his trousers, then he paused. 'Surely it can't be legal?'

'You bet it isn't. But who could prove anything against anyone without catching them redhanded? They aren't likely to find fingerprints.'

'Must be from Grimwick — that's easy enough to guess.'

I agreed. 'But Grimwick's a big place.'

As soon as Brandon was dressed and shaved we went up to The Clay & Wattle for coffee and toast. Outside his café we found Bill angrily at work cleaning the rustic wooden sign which told the world that coffee and teas and lunches were served here. His sticker said:

THEY SEEK HIM HERE, THEY SEEK HIM THERE
THEY SEEK FOR GRIMSBY EVERYWHERE
HE'S NOT IN RIDDLEFORD (SUCH A PITY)
SO LOOK FOR HIM IN GRIMSWICK CITY.

'It's not even clever,' Bill complained, 'and the glue they used is a bastard to get off. D'you imagine turps would do any good?'

But I couldn't help and nor could Brandon, so we went inside.

Staff and clientele alike were seething over this newest outrage, and Jane especially. As soon as she had a free moment she came over to sit with us, and we put our heads together and agreed that somebody must do something, and do it soon.

But who, and what?

XXXII

REACTIONS at the Foundation that morning seemed divided between those who thought the whole affair was something of a good joke on Riddleford and those who were indignant. But even those who were indignant were so only out of hurt pride. They came no nearer than the others to taking the matter seriously.

In the Seminar Room there was a deal of dilettante intellectual discussion. Someone proposed that the disagreement should be settled by plebiscite — 'In this democratic day and age,' he maintained, 'surely the Common Man should be permitted to decide for himself? Why should scholars and professors be allowed to make his mind up for him simply because their privileged position gives them access to more plentiful information?'

Another student was for combating Dr Nightly's theory by further, even more improbable hypotheses. 'Why don't we write a book proving that Nicolas Grimsby never existed at all — that he is simply a vegetation myth, left over from Druid rites once practised in the Riddle valley?'

'And the name of the town Grimwick,' another elaborated, 'is originally Grimsbywick — the town sacred to the cult-hero Grimsby.'

'Even if Nicolas Grimsby did exist,' said another, 'it is certainly not he who wrote the poems and plays. In fact they were written by Shakespeare, who couldn't publish them under his own name because his own name was being used by Bacon for *his* writings!'

'Don't forget that Shakespeare died five years before Nicolas Grimsby was born!' objected Phoebe Stuart-Stotts, ever the stickler for precise fact.

'Doesn't prove a thing, Phoebe. Everyone knows how untrustworthy our records are for that period. What happened was very likely this: there were in fact *two* Nicolas Grimsbys. And the one we know about, the Riddleford one (or the Grimwick one, if you believe Dr Nightly), isn't the same one as wrote the poems.'

And so it went on — elegant theories being bandied about from one to another. And all the time, I thought, someone somewhere is hatching out new plans and new plots which will end by destroying this Foundation of ours altogether.

Yet nobody was a whit more concerned when, later on in the day, I went round to the *Courant* offices. Alec had written a lead story on the stickers: Godfrey had taken several amusing photographs. Here, too, the general feeling seemed to be that it was something of a joke.

Alec had visited the Town Hall to ask Sam Hartpool what the Town Council thought of this new event and the outrage at The Birthplace.

'Juvenile delinquents — that's the official answer,' Alec said. 'I got treated to a complete sermon on today's irresponsible youth — did it for a lark, he says. Not like they were in his young days, it seems. He'd never have thought of doing a practical joke like that.'

'A pretty elaborate practical joke,' I remarked. 'And it wasn't done on the spur of the moment, either — those stickers had to be thought out and printed. Someone went to a lot of trouble and a lot of expense too. And the same with the paint on the statue.'

Alec nodded. 'Well, Geoff, I'm only telling you what Mr Hartpool said. He thinks they just seized on the excuse of Dr Nightly's book to get their own back on Riddleford. After all, there's always been any amount of friendly rivalry between the two towns.'

'And the Council thinks this is just a friendly practical joke, is that it? Between friends, sort of?' asked Gloria.

Alec said yes, that was it.

'Some friends,' said Gloria, and went back to her typing.

XXXIII

So Sam Hartpool, and Mr Grasmere, and all those who shared their view that anything which got Riddleford into the news was *ipso facto* a Good Thing, must have been highly delighted when a couple of days later the B.B.C. 'Tonight' television programme sent up one of their interviewers, a bearded and splendidly truculent Scot, with cameramen and engineers and the rest of the usual task force, to report to the nation on the latest development in the Nicolas Grimsby contest.

In a series of interviews with various key figures of the community, the interviewer established a remarkable absence of unanimity on the subject.

We learnt for the first time that the whole affair was a communist plot from start to finish when an elderly green-grocer was interviewed. Asked why he was so sure it was the communists, he said that he'd read in some American book about how the communists were always claiming to have invented everything first, like gravity and the atom bomb and the sputnik: and how like them it was to pretend Nicolas Grimsby was a communist. Asked if in fact anyone had suggested that Grimsby was a communist, he said, well, perhaps they hadn't said so in so many words, but that was the way they operated, see, they didn't come out in the open and fight clean and fair, see, they used these underhand methods, you never knew where you were with them, see, they were that crafty.

The interviewer thanked him soberly and politely and next talked to a young milkman returning from his morning round. Was he alarmed at the situation in Riddleford? Yes, the young fellow said, yes, he certainly was alarmed. Why was he alarmed? Well, it was fascism cropping up again, wasn't it? How did he mean, fascism? Well, all this writing on walls, that was a fascist trick, wasn't it? Like those swastikas. That chap Mosley, that was down in Notting Hill—the milkman was willing to bet he was at the bottom of it all.

Next the interviewer to his obvious delight came across an outspoken Scot-hater, who declared that it stood out a mile that the Scottish Nationalists were behind these outrages. It was their sort of trick, like the Stone of Scone and all. The interviewer objected that Grimwick was no more in Scotland than Riddleford was. Ah, that was just the cunning of it, said the other. He declared that there existed a secret plan—no, he hadn't exactly seen it himself but he'd met a chap once in a pub who had—for Scotland to occupy a large portion of Northumberland. And if the interviewer could see that map he'd notice that Grimwick was in the part that the Scots planned to annex. Why were they so keen to lay hands on Nicolas Grimsby, though? Because they had no great writers of their own. What about Burns, and Scott, and Robert Louis Stevenson? The Scot-hater laughed contemptuously. 'Man,' he asked, 'have you ever tried to read any of them? You can't understand a blessed word they say!'

Finally, inevitably, the interviewer called upon old Sid Grimsby for his views. And Sid, needless to say, was not slow to air his objectionable opinions. 'Best thing that could possibly happen, it would be, if Grimwick took 'im over. Riddleford ought by rights to stick 'im on a golden platter and 'and 'im over with our compliments. It'd be the finest day in Riddleford's 'istory, that would, getting shot of that load of tripe.'

'So you see,' the interviewer summed up, turning to face the camera and his millions of viewers across the length and breadth of Britain, 'so you see, there doesn't seem to be exactly any fierce indignation among the people of Riddleford about what's happening. You and I might perhaps have imagined that the good folk hereabouts would be seriously disturbed at the threat that their poet might be snatched away from them, with all that that entails in the way of civic pride and — perhaps more important — trade and business. But no, not a bit of it. As we've seen, there are many views on *why* what's happening is happening, but no voice that I've heard today is concerned to *do* anything about it. The truth of the matter seems to be, doesn't it, that nobody in Riddleford could care very much less?'

And with his famous housewife-charming smile he wished us all goodnight.

XXXIV

'DAMN damn damn damn damn!' said Jane. 'Damn Riddleford and damn Mr Grasmere and damn the B.B.C. and damn Sid Grimsby and damn every damn person except Nicolas himself.'

We contemplated the blank television screen, which she had just switched off in her fury. More than ever we were determined that somebody must do something, and do it soon.

But again, who, and what?

'If anyone can do anything,' said Jane, 'it's Hilda Bunting!'

'Very well,' I agreed. 'We'll fix up a meeting and talk the whole thing over with her.'

So I phoned Mrs Bunting up and said, briefly, what we felt: that Riddleford was letting itself be made a laughing-stock of the country, and it was time we started taking things seriously.

'Geoff, my dear, that's the most heart-warming thing I've heard anybody say for days! I've been making myself more and more miserable as the days went by . . . that business of sticking those dreadful scraps of paper all over the town! Monstrous! But d'you know, when I asked old Sam Hartpool what he intended to do about it, all he said was that he thought of writing a letter to the Mayor of Grimwick, expressing his dismay at what had taken place and hoping that some action could be taken to restrain those who had done it from doing it again. . . . I ask you! Sam's a dear, and I'm very fond of him. But it's no earthly use looking to him for action at a time like this!'

So we agreed to meet informally and pool our thinking on the whole business. Mrs B suggested a round-table conference for the following evening — the table in question being the one in the back parlour of The Fox & Chicks. Joe Higgs was ever Mrs Bunting's stoutest ally: besides, she never liked to be too far from something to drink.

'And Joe's a fine man to have at our side if there's going to be a scrap,' she added.

'She's evidently prepared for action!' commented Jane when I'd put the receiver down and reported what had been said. 'I'm sure she's the right person to get things started.' We both of us felt that shoulders had been put to wheels, that wheels had been set turning.

XXXV

JOE winked across the counter as we came into the Public Bar just before closing time the following evening. Before we could order any drinks he pushed across a big gin for Jane and large scotches for Brandon and myself. 'On the house,' he grinned. 'Knock 'em back and then come back into the Snug.'

In the Snug we found Hilda and Harold Bunting, both with generous drinks before them. A moment later we heard Joe telling his missus to carry on clearing up without him, and then he himself joined us, entering the little room like a conspirator, closing the door softly behind him after peering carefully up and down the passage outside. One of the girls brought in a tray with an assortment of beverages.

'There we are,' said Joe, satisfied. He refilled all our glasses. 'Now we're snug as can be — snug in the Snug, eh? Everyone got what they want?'

We all said we had and raised our glasses to him.

'Right — then let's get down to business, as the actress said to the bishop.'

'Who's going to open the proceedings?' asked Hilda, the instincts of a lifetime of committees coming to the fore. She looked across at us. 'You started all this — it better be one of you people.'

We all looked at one another. Eventually Jane submitted. She cleared her throat, blushed a little, and began. 'Well, we thought, that is, Geoff and Brandon and I thought, that it's a shame that nobody seems to be doing anything about this Grimsby business. I mean — well, you know what's been going on, and I think it's awful, really, the way nobody seems to be doing anything about it. I mean, in next to no time you'll have people going to Grimwick because they think that's where he was born, and you can't blame them really, can you, after all, if that's what they're led to believe? Only nobody here seems to care a hoot, even though everything in Riddleford depends, sort of, on having the tourists come, and if they stop, well, *everything* would stop. Only nobody seems to think of that, somehow.'

At which point she came to a stop. Joe said, 'Hear, hear!' in a hearty landlordly voice and topped her glass up.

'Isn't that right, pet?' Jane said to me, a little tremulous after saying so much out of the blue. Everyone sat back satisfied, smiling at her and murmuring approval. 'Very well spoken, child,' approved Mrs B, and Joe filled her glass too. She put out her hand just as the gin reached the rim.

Harold leant forward and, as always with him, everyone shushed whatever they were saying when they sensed he was about to speak. 'I take it,' he said, in his low quiet voice, 'we're all agreed that, whether for cash or credit, we're out to keep Nicolas Grimsby come what may?'

'Of course,' said his wife, 'what else?'

'Even if, in fact, Grimsby *was* born in Grimwick?'

'Harold, my love, don't start romanticising. We haven't time to waste.'

'We must be certain of our footing.'

Brandon tactfully interrupted. 'Let's at any rate assume for the moment that Grimsby belongs to us. We still believe that, after all, don't we?'

'No need to cross our Rubicons until we come to them,' I agreed.

'Well then,' Harold continued, 'we're prepared to back up our belief, are we? Ready to take action if need be? Have we all thought what that might entail?'

'That's what we're here to debate, isn't it?' asked Brandon. 'Someone — we don't know who — is trying to get at Grimsby, and we've got to defend him. We *must* take action — any kind of action we think necessary. If we wait until something really decisive should happen, we'll wait till doomsday. Judging by what's happened so far, it will be a war of attrition — a series of little attacks, sapping at

our defences until one day we look round and can't see our
Nicolas any more. . . . We've got to be prepared to stand
by Nicolas whatever happens, till the last trump sounds and
the last ditch falls and the gutters of Riddleford are red with
the last drop of our blood. That's the way I see it.'

Dramatic silence. And then the dramatic silence was
shattered by a spectacular yell. A voice spoke from
apparently nowhere in blood-curdling tones. 'That's
fightin' talk where Ah comes from. Reckon youse the guy
to help scalp these yellow-livered coyotes! Let's you and
I shake on that, pard!'

'Oh my God,' groaned Harold Bunting fatalistically, and
poor Joe just about jumped from his seat as — from the
serving-hatch which led through into the Public Bar —
scrambled Scrubby Bunting.

'Sabrina Bunting!' said her mother in her magisterialest
voice, 'when I left the house you were neatly tucked up
in your bed and asleep. What do you think you are
doing?'

But before her mother had a chance to grab her, Scrubby
had made herself at home on the arm of Brandon's chair.
She looked around at us contentedly and said, 'Please don't
let me interrupt anything. I just felt that I should be here,
that's all. . . . Do go on.'

The first time in my life I saw Scrubby Bunting I wanted
to rub my eyes. It was like passing La Gioconda in the High
Street or standing behind the Venus de Milo in the fish-
monger's queue. For I had lived with her all my life. Most
of us have. All her twelve years Scrubby has been her
father's favourite model — presumably because she doesn't

cost him anything. My vegetarian aunt has a Bunting in her spare bedroom which shows Scrubby in her gym slip, puzzling over her homework. That was Harold's naturalistic stage, when he went around everywhere saying 'To Hell with all these Isms! One touch of Nature makes the whole world kin!' Poor Scrubby got herself done in all sorts of intimate situations — plaiting her pigtails in the morning, or pink and naked after her bath.

But there's also a surrealist Scrubby, posed by an opaque sea with a monstrous onion and a herd of melting telephones. The title — *Comme les jours s'écoulent* — is rather unhelpful. She was pink in daddy's pink period and mauve in his mauve period. She has been long and thin like Modigliani, skewy and wide-eyed like Kisling, everything from Impressionist to Expressionist, from Neo-Realist to just plain Dada. Most recently of all she posed for the Unknown Displaced Person, in the course of which most of her own person got displaced too, so that it was hard to understand why Harold thought he needed a model at all.

Just how Scrubby has survived to the age of twelve in the Bunting household is quite a mystery. Hers are the least parental parents I know — not at all the sort to spock her up out of *Teach Yourself Mothercraft* in the best modern manner. Perhaps she was brought up with the Afghans, like Romulus and Remus, lapping her Ken-L-Meet from the same bowl and wagging a lot for Winalot.

I once asked her how she came to be called Scrubby instead of Sabrina. 'Oh, that's quite easy,' she replied. 'I've been called it ever since kindergarten. They had this pupils' concert, you see, and we all had to be these trees and sway in the wind and shed our leaves while Miss Doodah at the piano played *Autumn Song* by J. Springfield Dobbs, and by the time they got to me all the proper trees had been bagged, so I had to be a shrub. And I've been called Shrubby and then Scrubby ever since. Loathsome, isn't it?'

It took us a moment to get back to where we were after Scrubby's invasion. There was no question of throwing her out — Scrubby was not the kind of girl you can do that to. If she was with us, she was with us to stay.

Joe started the ball rolling again. 'If it's action you want, you can stop worrying right now, man. I can get a bunch of the boys together any time you care to mention, can nip over to Grimwick and slap bloody great posters all over the shop, if that's what you want.'

Harold smiled. 'We'll remember that when the time comes, Joe. But we're still feeling our way at present. For one thing, we don't really know for certain who the enemy is yet, do we?'

'Harold's right, I'm afraid,' said Hilda, looking at her husband proudly like a school-teacher at a favourite pupil who has just shone before the Inspector. 'No use fighting an enemy when you're blindfolded and he's not. First things first, and our first job is to find out who we're up against.'

'We know whoever it is must be someone fairly big — someone with money,' said Harold. 'That film you people saw over at Grimwick — must have cost a great deal. Someone is evidently prepared to risk quite a large sum to prove Dr Nightly right.'

'Surely,' Jane pointed out, 'the point is, who stands to gain most if the book *is* right?'

'Who? Why, every blessed soul in Grimwick!' answered Joe. 'They'll all make a packet if the tourists start going there instead of here.'

'But it can't be the whole of Grimwick that's in this. It must be some individuals,' I said. 'And if the ordinary people of Grimwick are like the ordinary people of Riddleford, they couldn't care less one way or the other.'

'But as Joe's just said, everyone in Grimwick stands to win,' Jane objected.

'Just as everyone in Riddleford stands to lose a great deal at this moment,' I answered. 'Yet you don't see it bothering them. I really don't see this as a mass job: I'm sure there must be some individual, or some group, a small group, at the bottom of it.'

'Well, as Hilda says, we've got to find out the facts,' said Brandon. 'That's the first step on our agenda — everyone agree?'

We all agreed.

'Tell you what's just occurred to me,' said Hilda. 'Obviously all this began with Dr Nightly's book, didn't it? Well, then, why can't you scholars just prove his book wrong. Then the whole silly business would just fizzle out!'

Brandon laughed, kindly but a little patronisingly. 'If only we could, Hilda. But you see, it isn't really a question of *proof*. Nightly doesn't *prove* his case. His chain of argument's solid as far as it goes, but it doesn't go all the way. Sooner or later you have to make a little jump of faith. All his book does is talk you into making that little jump. There's nothing for us to disprove.'

'I wonder if Dr Nightly knew what he was starting,' Jane reflected.

'I'm sure he didn't,' said Harold. 'Not that it would affect him anyway. There he sits — probably at this very moment — in his college rooms in some ancient Oxford building, looking out over the green lawns to the river . . . spinning his clever ideas out, longer and thinner and more subtle. What's it to him what use we others make of his notions? He's like people who invent H-bombs and missiles: knowledge is what he's looking for, and if a few people's lives are chewed up in the process, well, chalk it all up to experience.'

'If you ask me, which I don't suppose you do, but anyway,' said Scrubby indignantly, 'it all sounds jolly stupid!'

'And if you ask *me*,' Jane added, 'it sounds like a big bluff. A moral tug-of-war. Whichever side tugs hardest gets Nicolas — and the tourists with him — irrespective of whichever side is really in the right.'

'That's the situation in a nutshell,' Harold agreed. 'So we must be sure that it's us who tugs hardest. We're all agreed on *that*, I'm sure?'

Naturally we were.

> '*Hand on bludie hand, let's seale*
> *Our grislie compact up,*'

quoted Brandon impressively.

'Did he really say "bludie"?' Scrubby asked.

'Of course.'

'Good for Old Nick!' Scrubby looked defiantly at her mother.

The meeting broke up. Everybody promised everybody else to think up lots and lots of marvellous ideas for saving Nicolas. And then, with a medley of goodnights, we all went our several ways into the town.

XXXVI

MR GRASMERE came into our office from his own. Nothing was ever allowed to disturb his serene imperturbability, but something had come perilously near it this morning. 'Geoff,' he said, 'hurry round to the Town Hall right away, will you?'

'What's up?'

'Some sort of a demonstration. Don't ask me who by or what against, because I don't know. Nobody seems to know. Godfrey's out on a job at the moment, but we've told him to get round there as soon as he can make it. In the meantime, get there fast as you can, will you?'

Two or three minutes later I was leaning my bike against the wall of the Town Hall. Something certainly seemed to be happening. On the pavement outside was a bevy of women, waving placards in a militant manner. The largest placard, supported by two especially hefty ladies, said:

RIDDLEFORD IS PURE — KEEP IT PURE

Smaller placards had messages to similar effect:

LET GRIMWICK KEEP ITS GRIME

RIDDLEFORD DOES NOT NEED GRIMWICK'S DIRT

I sneaked into the building by the side entrance and wound my way to the main lobby. Tim Robson the porter was standing there undecidedly in his municipal uniform, looking out on to the sunlit pavement where more and more aggressive women were gathering. 'What's it all about, Tim?' I asked.

Tim turned to me, relieved to find another male in the neighbourhood. 'It's you, is it, Geoff? Well, I really don't know as I could say *what* it is, exactly. But this I *can* tell you: one lady she came in to ask if Mr Hartpool was upstairs, and I didn't know what to say, so I said yes, he was. . . . She didn't ask if he was free or would he see them or anything, you see, just if he was upstairs. . . . So it must be him they're after, but what it is they're after him for they won't say. . . . They're all there, though, every bleeding nosy parker in Riddleford. . . . And, by God, there's Miss Jobling herself! I said to myself, *she* can't be far away!'

And now I saw her myself, moving through the gathering and creating little squalls wherever she went. It was characteristic. Miss Jobling buzzes round Riddleford like a sharp-nosed speedboat, and she leaves so much wash fanning out behind her that even people far away know all about it.

Whatever happens in Riddleford — a Relief Fund for Flooded Finns or a Pageant of Woman Through The Ages or an amateur production of *Song of Norway* in the Church Hall or a Jumble for the natives of Borioboola-Gha on the left bank of the Niger — in all these pies, if you don't find Hilda Bunting's finger you'll find Miss Jobling's. If the Armenians run short of blankets or the inhabitants of Botany Bay need Balaclava helmets, somehow word is passed round the globe to Miss Jobling, and somehow Miss Jobling sees that something is done.

Nor are her missionary efforts wholly directed *outside* the community. Who but Miss Jobling keeps an eye on the goings-on that go on of a Saturday night in the shrubberies of Potter's Path, and reports to the Council in vivid detail the result of her torchlit research? Have you noticed that we in Riddleford don't have our Sabbaths desecrated in the filthy Continental manner by cricket on the green and such-like debaucheries: who do you think we have to thank for that?

How is it, again, that more books have been banned by Riddleford County Library than any other local authority in the country? For years, too, Miss Jobling prevented Mixed Bathing at the Municipal Baths. And when, over her all-but-dead body, they relaxed the regulations, she saw to it that at any rate the tatters of the decencies were respected — the rules go into microscopic anatomic detail over the amount of flesh that one is allowed to display.

The only factor which compensates for this embattled puritanism on Miss Jobling's part is Hilda Bunting. I forget how the two of them first met in battle — some misty legend is still recounted in the pubs, of fantastic complexity, concerning licences and the young and the Demon Alcohol. I know that Joe Higgs was mixed up in it somewhere, and that it was then that the old alliance between him and Mrs Bunting began. But what the cause of the dispute was, and who was fighting for what, nobody seems to remember for sure: all are agreed that it was a famous victory, but none recalls who in fact was victorious. What is certain is that ever since then Mrs Bunting and Miss Jobling have been at daggers drawn.

And now, like Liberty Leading The People of the French Revolution but with not quite so much bosom on display, here she was. She led her private army up the steps of the Town Hall and halted it in the lobby. They all looked expectantly up at the green-and-cream staircase, thirsting for the blood of the Chairman of the Urban District Council.

When he did in fact appear the ladies surged towards him like the French Revolutionaries surrounding a hapless aristo who has been foolish enough to repeat some stale jest about bread and cake. I felt very sorry for him.

'Yes, Miss Jobling,' asked Sam wearily, 'what is it *this* time?'

Miss Jobling stared at him for a moment to show she wasn't to be cowed by this unwelcome. Then she started to explain her mission. Scribbling as hard as I could, my short-hand could only just keep up with her:

Did Mr Hartpool and his fellow-members of the Council imagine, Miss Jobling — and here he was to understand that Miss Jobling spoke not only for herself but for the assembled

women of Riddleford, who had done her the honour of
asking her to be their spokeswoman today — would like
to know, that the proud honour of Riddleford's matrons
and maids could be trampled in the dust as though they
mattered not a scrap? Did neither reputation nor common
decency evoke a response in their blind hearts? Were they
deaf to all things noble, seemly and of good repute? Did
it not behove him, whom this town had elected to be
mentor, guide of its conduct and overseer of its moral
behaviour, to raise his hand against all sign and token of
vice, rather than allow all that was true and pure and beautiful to be dragged in the slime? Was this the way in which
he repaid their trust, who had chosen him in the faith that
the sanctity of their family life was secure in his hands? Yes,
Miss Jobling called upon Mr Hartpool to answer, or no?

Sam had obviously lost his hold on Miss Jobling's thread
several sentences ago: and now he was confronted with a
direct question which he simply did not understand. Nor
was it simply a flourish of rhetoric, a pause for emphasis
and puff. Miss Jobling wanted an answer. She stood glaring
at him, her hair a little distrait, her meagre bosom rising and
falling heavily.

Poor Sam hovered for a moment, then plunged. It was,
after all, a fifty-fifty chance. 'Yes,' he replied.

Miss Jobling positively snarled in triumph. She turned
to her supporters, who looked admiringly back at their
leader.

'Mr Chairman,' Miss Jobling exclaimed, 'please be so
good as to cast your eyes over *this*!'

One of her underlings handed a wispy leaflet to Sam, who
started fishing for his reading glasses. Others were handed

to the two other Council members who were waiting in the background in case Sam needed help.

Miss Jobling recognised me for the first time. 'Give him one,' she told the woman. 'I trust Mr Grasmere will see fit to take notice of this in the *Courant*.'

The leaflet which I now read was a very ingenious piece of work.

It was addressed to the Housewives of Riddleford. The writer admitted that they would probably find it shocking. It was a painful duty that he had to perform, he told them, but one that he would not shirk, for this was a time for plain speaking. He felt the need to acquaint the people of Riddleford with the sort of 'literature' their Nicolas Grimsby had written.

Did they know what subtle poison was being injected into the impressionable minds of their sons and daughters at school?

Did they know what vicious teachings were perverting their youth and corrupting their innocence, all in the name of art, that cloak which hid such blight, such mildew?

In case they did not, the leaflet proceeded to examples.

It had not been difficult for the anonymous author to find weapons for his crusade. Most of Grimsby's output is concerned with his favourite topic — Love. And by love he meant love with no holds barred. We're a long way here from the soft romantic effusions of later ages, all breathing human passion far above. The word sentimental had not been coined in Grimsby's day: love in his verse is sex, naked and unashamed, breathing very loud indeed.

Naturally this is apt to disturb those of us who have been brought up by the Sunday newspapers to believe that all sex is wicked. Not that Nicolas is ever actually coarse: he's too good a poet for that. It's a matter of *honi soit qui mal y pense.* You'd have to be easily offended indeed to object to the epigram on Mistress Sarah Cutts which was quoted in the leaflet:

> *Sara's not Vile, yet likes she Viols best,*
> *When twixt her legs the Instrument doth rest.*

The leaflet also quoted one of the Epistles, *Love's Siege*:

> *While yet the Hands, those cunning Spyes, doe trye*
> *The battel-ground, where he must shortlie lye,*
> *Armd for the Fight, my Souldiour stifflie standes,*
> *Impatient of the order to aduance.*
> *The Prospect of his Foe dismaies him not,*
> *But rather makes him for the Fight more hot.*
> *What tho his Enemies hold throwe him downe,*
> *Dropping his head whenas the Victorie's won?*
> *A moment will his former heighth restore*
> *And send him forth as reddie as before.*
> *Corage reneued will make him new to swell*
> *And seeke again the deep-trenched Citadell.*
> *But now with desperate Stroke hele fight no more,*
> *His enemie receiues her Conquerour.*
> *The gates stand open now the Breech is seised,*
> *Henceforth the more he comes the more shees pleasd.*

I had to admit that a dozen of such poems, collected together, did make rather startling reading. Sam was standing with a very red face, peering through his reading glasses:

153

very likely this was the first time he had learnt of this new side to his town's native poet.

'You'd best tell me where you got this, Miss Jobling,' he said, folding up the leaflet and looking at his waiting opponent.

'This morning a copy of this filth was pushed through nearly every letterbox in Riddleford, Mr Chairman,' she replied.

I wondered why my cottage had been left off the mailing list. Perhaps the leaflets had been distributed after the normal post, so as to reach the more vulnerable housewife after hubbie had left for work.

'Almost every wife and mother in the town — unmarried girls too,' she went on, 'has been subjected to this indignity! Her eyes blazed with indignation. 'It is your duty to remedy the evils of this outrage. This vile monster is the poet that we have been brought up to admire and respect! At this very moment our children are sucking in this draught of abomination!'

Miss Jobling's words drew a sympathetic murmur from her followers. But Sam stood firm. 'Now, Miss Jobling, let's take a look at the facts, shall we?'

Miss Jobling said nothing, waiting to see what the Chairman's idea of facts was before she would commit herself. 'Nicolas Grimsby is famous all over the world,' Sam reminded her. 'Everyone's heard of him, wherever you go. Well, you know, Miss Jobling, it isn't for the likes of you and me to go setting ourselves up against the rest of the world, now, is it?'

'Whether he's the greatest poet in the world or not has nothing to do with it, Sam Hartpool. If his poetry is unfit for the wives and daughters of the town — and the men-folk, too, though perhaps they're so far gone it makes no difference what they read or don't read — then it matters not though he's the finest poet who ever set pen to paper. If the scholars and clever men think that a man who can write such filth as this is a great poet, they ought to have their heads examined. More shame to them, say I, and so say all decent-minded Englishwomen!'

She looked round for support from her backers. Cries of 'Aye, that's right!' came, and a solitary shout of 'Give it to 'em, hinny!'

Emboldened by this demonstration of solidarity, Miss Jobling made her declaration. Planting her feet firmly in front of the Chairman, she said emphatically, 'Mr Hartpool, you must renounce Nicolas Grimsby!'

'What's that?' Sam was really shocked.

'You must tell the world we have no need of such a man. I believe the people of Grimwick have got it into their heads that Nicolas Grimsby was in fact a citizen of their town, not ours. If so, they are welcome to him, and all his filth with him. For our part, we want no part of him.'

Sam just gawked at her. The assembled ladies moved as one body a step nearer and raised their banners yet higher. I began to fear that Sam didn't know his way out of this mess.

I was wrong. Sam Hartpool hadn't been elected Chairman for nothing.

After considering for a moment he jerked his head up and stared straight at Miss Jobling. 'That's very interesting,' he said. 'I am sure, Miss Jobling, and all your ladies, I am sure I am saying what my colleagues on the Council would wish me to say, when I say we are very grateful for the service you have rendered the ratepayers of Riddleford in giving up of your valuable time to bring this to our notice. .... I have no doubt there's a great deal in all what you've been saying. But as you'll be the first to appreciate, Miss Jobling, it is not for me to take it on myself, in defiance of what's laid down by the law of this land, to give you any sort of undertaking whatsoever. The question will need to be placed in the regular manner before the Council, and until then I can't offer any opinion. You'll just have to wait and see whether the Council feels called upon to perform any such action as this what you want. It could be, Miss Jobling, that they will: on the other hand' — he gazed at a distant wall — 'it could equally well be that they will not.'

Miss Jobling looked icicles at him. Then without another word she turned on her heels and led her cohorts out into the street. Sam stood there, his hands in his pockets, rocking with silent laughter as the doors swung to behind the last of the women of Riddleford. His colleagues looked at him with starry-eyed admiration.

'Man,' said the Chairman, wiping his mouth with the back of his hand, 'could I use a drink! That Miss Jobling, she gives you a thirst.'

And there the matter had, for the time being, to be left to hang to dry.

XXXVII

'WWow!' exclaimed Brandon, leaning back in my
kitchen chair. 'So old Sam gave Miss Jobling her
comeuppance, did he? Good for him!' He picked
up again the leaflet which lay on the table among leftovers of lunch. 'Neat job of work.'

We were both agreed that, whatever the high-minded
writer of the leaflet might say in his preface, his concern was
not really with the morals of Riddleford. To us it seemed
clear that here we had yet another Machiavellian move in
the Grimsby-for-Grimwick campaign — an ingeniously
hypocritical device to create a Fifth Column within Riddleford itself, by persuading such susceptible souls as Miss
Jobling and her companions to voluntarily relinquish their
claim to Nicolas Grimsby.

'Whoever thought this up,' Brandon remarked, pouring
himself another tumbler of beer, 'was nobody's fool. Right
on the ball.'

'It's nothing more than copying the poems out of the
books,' I said. 'Anyone could do it.'

'Think so?' Brandon pushed the leaflet across the table
to me. 'Read the text of that poem there. See if you notice
anything.'

I read it while Brandon peeled himself an apple and
crunched it. It was the poem Grimsby wrote about *A Distant Prospect of Belinda Disrobing* in which he hints, not

over-subtly, that a less distant prospect would be even more gratifying.

I didn't notice anything special about it, and said so.

'If you spent less time with that rag of yours and more at the Foundation,' he said, 'you'd be a little less woefully ignorant on matters scholastic. . . . Take another look at the text.'

I obeyed, but it didn't seem to help any.

'It's the 1758 text of the pirated edition printed in Antwerp. Remember that Project we did on textual variations? Well, this cropped up then. It's quite different from the version in the standard Collected Works.'

I considered it for a moment and then agreed. I hacked myself off a slice of cheddar while I contemplated the implications.

'Suggestive, isn't it?' said Brandon. He leant forward eagerly. 'How many copies of the Antwerp edition are there in the country? Two or three at most. The only other place you'd find this version is in the Variorum Edition, where all the variants are printed so you can compare them. Well, who'd have a Variorum Edition — or even access to one? Only a scholar, isn't that so?'

'So it looks as though we have a real genuine expert working against us?'

'That seems to be the long and short of it.'

XXXVIII

TALKING with the others a day or two later, I suggested we might simply reprint the leaflet and have it pushed through every letterbox in Grimwick: it would at least restore the status quo. 'Then Mayor Duncible will have to put up with the same sort of trouble as poor old Sam,' said Jane. 'The housewives of Grimwick won't want Nicolas any more than the housewives of Riddleford.'

'It's not quite the same,' said Brandon. 'There's no Miss Jobling in Grimwick.'

'Shows how little you still know about England,' I said. 'There isn't a city or town or village in this country without its own private particular Miss Jobling. She's a local institution without which English culture as we know it couldn't survive.'

'Fair enough. Then why don't we go ahead with this scheme?'

But Harold Bunting had the answer to that. 'There's nothing to be gained by calling names back when someone calls you names. Especially in this instance. Who gets hurt most by this leaflet? Nicolas, of course. There would be a small victory if we did succeed in persuading the good women of Grimwick that they should reject him just as their sisters of Riddleford are disposed to do, but it would be a tactical victory only. Strategically it would be a defeat, because it would be a defeat for Nicolas. Don't let us forget that we're fighting this battle not just to preserve the sacred prosperity of Riddleford, but to save Nicolas for *himself*. Otherwise it will be like two nations fighting over a piece of land which at the end of the war is so battle-scarred that it isn't worth possessing.'

We felt chastened. 'So what we have to do,' I asked, 'is something *positive* — we have to change the minds of *our* housewives, not the housewives of Grimwick?'

'That's more like it.'

Hilda Bunting knew what should be done. 'I know, I'll go round and have a quiet word with the Rector,' she said. She wouldn't say any more. Afterwards Brandon suggested that perhaps she planned to have the Church curse Grimwick with bell, book and candle, and bring down the Seven Plagues of Egypt on its godless citizenry.

But it was nothing so dramatic. Mrs B warned me to be at Saint Bridget's for matins the following Sunday, and so I heard him preach. Taking as his text *'They that are after the flesh do mind the things of the flesh but they that are after the spirit the things of the spirit Romans eight five'*, his sermon was virtually a whitewashing of Grimsby. He made no direct reference to the leaflets, but he left no doubt in our minds what he was referring to. We were warned not to judge the people of past ages by the standards of today. He spoke of changing values, and suggested that some scheming gentry might seek to exploit them for their own dubious purposes. As if by chance, he gave us as example the poems of Nicolas Grimsby. There were those, he was aware, who considered that perhaps his lovely verses were a little outspoken for this present day and age. But we should not allow that to influence our minds against the sublime poet of whom we were, were we not, so justly proud. . . .

Riddleford is not an especially church-going town, but the effects of the Rector's sermon spread to a far wider audience than that of Saint Bridget's congregation. My report in the *Courant* was generously featured by Mr Grasmere under the banner headline:

RECTOR LASHES HUMBUGS
Saint Bridget's hears blow
struck against mealy-mouths

Miss Jobling's supporters came back to their senses. Little by little the movement died a natural death, and the chalked slogans of 'GRIMSBY GO HOME' were gradually washed off the walls of the Public Library and the railway arch by the kindly deterging rain.

XXXIX

IN the course of another conversation, 'Distinguished patronage!' Mrs Bunting exclaimed, taking a hint from one of her many committees' reports, where the list of patrons was led by many aristocratic titles. 'Now, there's something we could do with a spot of!'

Personally I was not convinced that snobbery works wonders any longer, but Brandon was sure the Great British Public loved a title as dearly as ever. He was enthusiastic when Hilda proposed that he and I should go over to

Gooseleigh to see if we could interest Lord Otterburn in what was happening in his bailiwick. An appointment was made, and a few afternoons later we took the little local bus from Riddleford.

Gooseleigh has been the seat of the Gooses since goodness knows when, and has the interesting distinction of being one of the few Border strongholds which have never been burned to the ground. The reason is quite simple — the Gooses have the longest and most consistent record of sitting on the fence of any family in Burke or Debrett.

Through long centuries of Border raids and inter-baronial skirmishes the Gooses have kept wonderfully, successfully quiet. When they have emerged from their fastness it has only been when they were absolutely certain who was Top Dog. During the Wars of the Roses they stayed at home till Henry landed, whereupon their retainers mingled with the victorious army and convinced everyone that they had been there from the start — earning their lords and masters a fair-sized chunk of royal gratitude. Then during the seventeenth century — in the lifetime of that Cranbourn Goose who may or may not have been Grimsby's father — the Gooses were moderately Royalists, but with a tinge of serious interest in the new political theories which caused the Commonwealth to eye them favourably — perhaps they might be converted to the Parliamentary cause? This never quite happened, but so nearly that the family fortunes gained rather than lost during that period when so many other noble houses were ruined.

And so over the centuries the house of Goose has climbed rung by rung. Their final promotion was thanks to William IV, at a time when it seemed to His Majesty's Ministers that a stronghold of established aristocracy in the North might stave off some of the worst excesses of the Industrial Revolution. Why the Gooses? Perhaps quite simply because they felt that no family could survive so long without deserving some reward.

The Stately Home of Gooseleigh began life as humbly as the family itself — little more than a fortified farmhouse, just as the Gooses themselves were little more than glorified farmers. As the family grew in station so did their castle in stature — a tower here, a lodge there, a wing on the south, a terrace on the west. . . .

Today the splendours of Gooseleigh are a little faded from the day when, less than a century ago, Augustus Hare could pay for his board and lodging by calling Gooseleigh 'perhaps the happiest of the country homes, although one of the most draughty, at which I stayed in this part of England'. The draughts remain, but gone is the day when visitors came from all over the country to stay at Gooseleigh, and Lord Otterburn was regarded by all Northumbria as its divinely authorised liege lord.

Yet the great lawns still sweep down beside the drive — those same lawns where, a hundred years ago, pale girls minced languidly in their crinolines, accompanied by slim-waisted men who paid them elegant court and perhaps — who knows? — enticed them into the shrubberies to bestow a kiss behind a goose-shaped box hedge?

And it was beneath those superb chestnuts which still dominate the approach that Anatole de Cluny wrote the exquisite lines that so turned the head of Miriam Goose, in those bliss-filled days before 1870 when life was empty of

Prussians and sabre-rattlers and an impoverished French poet could have a truly delightful time as a French tutor in an English Stately Home . . . and it was here, too, that Anatole was caught behaving in a most indelicate manner with the German governess, sending Miriam into a decline from which she never recovered, English daughters in Stately Homes at that time not having been told about such things, and causing Monsieur Anatole to be packed home to his native Lyons as fast as the handsome new railway could take him.

In those days the Railway was the Newcastle, Grimwick, Riddleford & Alston Line, not simply British Railways (N.E.). There was a halt in the grounds where visitors coming to Gooseleigh — and foreign poets leaving — could have the train stopped specially for them.

That never happens today. Today the diesels rattle past and only the most knowledgeable of the bored passengers gazing from their windows can identify the crenellated turrets above the trees. . . . Today there is willow-herb in the drive, and the Agent wants to sell the chestnuts for timber, and the lawns are spattered with plantains, and there are molehills all over the tennis court.

But that didn't stop Brandon and me feeling pretty small as we came scrunching up the drive.

XL

THE place was so overgrown that I felt like the Prince come to pay his respects to the Sleeping Beauty. The front door was virtually concealed behind ivy like an Old English Sheepdog. After poking about for a bit we came across a bell-pull. I gave it a tug and after a moment we heard a distant tinkling in some remote scullery. 'The speed of sound is much slower in these old houses,' Brandon explained.

Silence refell. Then we heard, far away, someone coming. The sound of bolts being drawn, of handles pulled from within, and the huge door swung slowly open. We turned to speak to the portly butler — but there wasn't a portly butler there at all, only a small child, probably female but we couldn't be certain.

'Did you want anyfing?' it asked.

'We'd like to see Lord Otterburn if we may.'

The child opened its eyes wide. 'Oh Christ!' it said. 'Oh dearie Christie me! You see, Dad's asleep!'

'Well, he's expecting us — I phoned him yesterday. D'you think he'll wake up soon?'

The child looked at us as if we were crazy. 'It's me dad that's asleep. Slordship's in the garding gardning.'

'Well, then,' said Brandon, 'we could go round and see him, couldn't we? You could show us where he is?'

'Oh never never! Never at all in your life you can't do that!' Tears came into the poor thing's eyes as it contemplated the enormity of Brandon's suggestion. It looked at me as if hoping I would hold him back, but it was out of luck.

'Don't worry,' I said, 'we'll be all right.'

We started to walk round to the back of the house, and the child whined 'But what'll I say to Dad?' and then even fainter 'And what'll Dad say to me?' but by that time we were past caring.

The head of the House of Goose was hoeing lettuces as we approached, but — the afternoon being warmish — seemed glad enough to stop and rest on his hoe. We introduced ourselves and he gave up work altogether and retrieved his jacket from a redcurrant bush which had been holding it for him like a well-trained lackey.

He mopped his face with a grey handkerchief. 'Y'know,' he said, 'there's one thing I think I'd best make clear right from the start, gentlemen: we aren't very fond of poets here in Gooseleigh.' He looked at each of us sharply to see how we took that.

'No?' asked Brandon uncertainly.

'We'll go in, shall we? . . . No, they talk too much, don't you know, and do so little. Odd fellers. We had one here, you know, Frenchman. Used to write poems about what he got up to with the womenfolk — extraordinary stuff. We've got some of his things upstairs in the library — curious, if you like that kind of thing. Some do, some don't, I know.'

He led us into the house. While tea was preparing he showed us round the house — which, as Brandon remarked afterwards, did at least save us half-a-crown, so we did get *something* out of our trip. But set against that was the fact that Lord Otterburn was very ill-informed about his family — didn't know half the facts and anecdotes about them that the regular guide did.

When tea was served he explained that Lady Otterburn was away opening a bazaar — 'Always opening things,' he said. 'I suppose these affairs close as well as open, but one never seems to hear about it.' So there were just the three of us for tea, sitting round a small table in the huge library. To judge by the stewedness, the tea was the same wretched brew as his kitchen provided for the half-crown visitors: the cake was hard as nails.

We did our best to get the conversation round to Nicolas, but the old man always seemed to lose the thread and switch to some other topic. Poets . . . that reminded him of Anatole de Cluny. He must show us those poems. . . .

They were all that he had promised: I shuddered to think what they might be worth, unpublished erotica by perhaps the most celebrated of French Impressionist poets. That German governess must have been quite a girl, too, by the sound of it. . . .

> *Quand je tiens en mes bras une géante molle*
> *Dont les très ardents doigts*
> *Impurs*
> *Parcourent les endroits*
> *Obscurs*
> *En la pine évoquant une ardeur enfin folle. . .*

and much more to the same effect.

The poems led to a discussion on whether there was something in the Riddleford air which led to this kind of verse. . . .
But Lord Otterburn pointed out that this was quite different
from Nicolas Grimsby's — 'The French do these things so
well, don't they? Our Nicolas was only a fumbling
amateur, compared to this. . . .' Brandon tried to suggest
that there was more to poetry, even poetry about sex, than
a play-by-play description of intimate events, but our host
seemed oblivious to any other criteria. . . .

From Anatole's ecstasies we passed to anecdotes of the
neighbourhood: what he didn't know about the private
lives of the local bigwigs wasn't worth knowing. After an
hour of his scandals we would have credited anything —
would have believed Colonel Jonson-Platt capable of
embezzling the Rugby Club funds or Mr Dwindle
capable of celebrating the Black Mass as his predecessor —
so Lord Otterburn assured us — had regularly celebrated it.

'Funny old coot,' Brandon commented as we bussed
home again.

'Nice old bird,' I agreed.

And it was not till we were back in Riddleford that we
realised how artfully the old dodger had diverted us from
the object of our mission. Once again the Gooses were
sitting tight on their fence.

XLI

'WHAT did you think of Auntie Muriel this week?' I asked Jane one evening at home.

Jane looked at me puzzled. 'Who's Auntie Muriel? It doesn't sound like anyone I know.'

'Auntie Muriel in the *Courant*. You know, Jim, in the Children's Page.'

'Oh, *him*!' Her mind clicked. 'I never read it. Why, have I missed something?'

'So you don't know about the private war he's having with Uncle George?'

'Who's Uncle George?'

'Auntie Muriel's opposite number on the *Grimwick Clarion*. In fact it was really her who started it off.'

'Who, Auntie Muriel?'

'No, Uncle George. He's really a she, you know.'

'I didn't, but go on, it's fascinating.'

I ignored her sarcasm and did go on. 'Well, as I say, it was really Uncle George who started it off. She told her kiddies that Nicolas didn't really live in Riddleford but in Grimwick, and she told them to tell this to their little Riddleford friends, and they weren't to play with any nasty little Riddleford kiddies who didn't believe them. And she had a lot of badges made — you know how children love pinning badges all over themselves — with a picture of Nicolas and the letters G.F.G. on them.'

'What does G.F.G. mean?'

'That's their war-cry: GRIMSBY FOR GRIMWICK!'

'The things they think of!' Jane marvelled. 'It'll be babes in arms next, they'll be brainwashing them while they're asleep in their cradles.'

'Auntie Muriel said that in his opinion Uncle George should be ashamed of herself. Starting fights between the kids and all. And Uncle George said Auntie Muriel should be ashamed of *him*self, asking children to go on believing lies. So this week Auntie Muriel said Uncle George should go and jump in the river.'

'And has she?'

'Not up till now, but you never know.'

XLII

IT was my turn to receive information a few days later. I was cycling happily along Grimsby Street towards the Foundation when I all but ran full tilt into Scrubby on her bike coming out of Scholars Alley — she being mounted dangerously on a fiercely flamboyant model appropriately called *Pink Witch*. With a nasty squeak and a smell of singed rubber we braked in time not to add to the month's accident statistics.

'I was hoping I'd run into you,' she said.

'You jolly nearly succeeded,' I replied.

'You know what I mean. . . . Have you heard about Mr

Jones — Fothergill Jones the Guide, I mean? The one who looks like a lizard?'

'What about him?'

'He's been sacked.'

'Look,' I said, 'I'm supposed to be a reporter. That means I'm supposed to know everything that happens in this town. How come you know so much more about everything than I do?'

'Well, you see, Mummy hears everything that goes on in Riddleford. Naturally. And so I only have to keep my ears open and I get to hear everything too. I heard all about Mr Jones yesterday evening, when I was supposed to be doing my Latin prep.'

'And what exactly did you hear?'

'Apparently he started telling the people he was being a guide to that it wasn't really true, all that he was saying. He told them that Nicolas was really born in Grimwick, and they were wasting their time and money coming to Riddleford, they ought to go *there* instead!'

'Blimey! Who found out about this?'

'One of the visitors came into the Information Office saying he thought it was perfectly damnable what was going on, Riddleford enticing visitors to come here when Grimsby wasn't a Riddleford person at all. So of course the Information people sent someone to listen to what Mr Jones was saying, dressed up as a sightseer, you know. And it was true. So they told Mummy, and Mummy told the Council, and they took away his licence and said he better get away from Riddleford pretty damn quick or he'd never live to tell the tale.'

'I should think not,' I said. 'Has he gone?'

'I wouldn't know. But I expect so. I mean, people would tar and feather him if he stayed — isn't that what they do? Mummy's always saying people should be tarred and feathered. . . . Mummy says, though, he may have done an awful lot of harm already. I mean, we don't know how long he's been saying this kind of thing, do we?'

'What are they going to do about it, anything?'

'Daddy thinks they ought to spread the rumour that Mr Jones went off his rocker and they've shut him up in a loony bin. That would stop the visitors being suspicious, wouldn't it?'

'Good idea as any. . . . Do they know if he was being paid to say this or just doing it off his own bat?'

'I think he must have been being paid, don't you? He always looked the sort of man who wouldn't do a thing unless it was for money.'

'As far as I'm concerned, Grimwick is welcome to him.'

It was difficult to believe, looking at Riddleford going about its normal life, that there was a war being waged. The visitors came and went quite happily, and only isolated incidents like the Jones business, the Birthplace Statue business, the Uncle George business, reminded us that the tug-of-war was actually in progress. The Press, radio, television made intermittent references to the dispute, but it wasn't eventful enough to keep in the public eye for long. Even in Riddleford, where events loomed larger in perspective, it was easy for us to forget that at any moment Nicolas might be lost to us altogether.

But when we went into Grimwick there were other reminders. At every visit we saw yet another Ye Olde

Grimsbie Tea Shoppe or Grimsby Petrol Station. The former Railway Arms became The Poet's Head. The Woolacombe Guest House was transformed into Grimsby's Nook. And finally a new housing estate was christened by Mrs. Duncible the Mayor's wife — christened Grimsby Gardens, with every one of its streets and crescents named for one of the characters in his plays.

'If only one of us could think of something!' Scrubby sighed. And there was little one could do but sigh with her.

XLIII

You would have thought that with all these goings-on they would not have had the nerve to hold the Annual Cricket Match between Riddleford and Grimwick. I said as much one day at the office, when Jim happened to be there.

'Think so?' he replied. 'Man, they wouldn't dare *not* hold it! If they cancelled it they'd be admitting something was wrong, like. And if something was wrong, they'd have to do something, like. So it's easier all round just to shut their eyes.'

And so Officialdom shut its eyes and everything went smoothly forward for The Match of the Season.

I don't know what your picture is of cricket — *real* cricket, I mean, not the souped-up county stuff that goes by the same name. Perhaps you picture the Village Green . . .

the blacksmith's demon bowling . . . the Vicar's quiet jokes and his subtle off-spins . . . the Squire square-jawed as he buckles on his pads . . . the Squire's pretty daughter in her flowered dress, sunbonnet and parasol, smiling at young Frank, the Hope of the Side, as he goes into battle for the honour of the Village . . . the Captain saying strong silent things to the Eleventh Man as he goes in to make the last runs needed for victory . . . the breathless hush . . . the last over . . . the fading light when the Umpire's white coat stands out like a ghost . . . day falling behind the poplars . . . the cry of first slip . . . swallows skimming six inches off the ground . . . the last ball.

Was the Riddleford-Grimwick match anything like that? Strangely enough, yes. The enthusiasm, the sense of occasion, were there in full measure. For weeks beforehand the match was the main topic of conversation wherever men gathered. In the Public Bar, under the barber's towel, on street corners before opening time, during the lunch-break at the Sanitary Drainpipe Company, over tea and muffins at the Rectory — everywhere it was of the match they spoke. And the members of the team went about the daily round, the common task, like tribal braves marked out for sacrifice and apotheosis.

This year, as you might expect, the anticipation doubled that of other years, and a double weight of responsibility lay on the shoulders of the players. And as the eyes of Riddleford turned towards its team, so the hopes of the team turned towards its Umpire.

Brandon found it hard to appreciate the role of the Umpire in local cricket. Yes, it was true, I explained, that the Riddleford Umpire interpreted the rules in what might be thought a loose sort of way . . . yes, perhaps some might call it cheating. But just the same was true of the Grimwick Umpire. And then there are limits beyond which cheating is considered indefensible — but how explain this shadowy line of demarcation between what the Umpire could and what he could not hope to get away with?

There must always be room for doubt, perhaps that was it. With whatever appearance of accident, a batsman should not strike the wicket-keeper with his bat, no matter how imminent the danger of being stumped. Again, it's asking too much for the wicket-keeper to dislodge the bails and make his appeal before the ball has left the bowler's hand. . . .

'I guess it's something instinctive,' Brandon decided after I had done my best to expound and failed. 'You have to be born and bred to it. But I do see that the Umpire is a very important member of the team.'

Perhaps on the great day itself the players would have observed that delicate but all-important moral frontier if they had been allowed to play the game in their own way. But they weren't.

It was played on the Ezekiah Routledge Memorial Ground at Grimwick, out past the slaughterhouse. Brandon and I went along with Jim who was covering the event for the *Courant*. He told us he'd never seen such a turn-out. It was always a well-supported game, but this year was out of the ordinary. As we looked out across the field from the Press seats, Jim added, 'Pretty excited too, if you ask me, man. They're always a noisy shower, but this is noisier than most. Shouldn't be surprised if we don't have a spot of trouble before the day's over and done with.'

Jim was proved right sooner than he expected. Just as the two captains were deciding the toss, and the coin was flipped spinning into the air, a Riddleford supporter yelled, 'Smash the ruddy sods, Jockie!'

I don't suppose Jock Winch, our captain, so much as heard the advice. But a couple of Grimwick men promptly set on the Riddleford enthusiast, who looked rather the worse for drink. They were giving him a rough pasting when a pair of policemen arrived, elbowing through the amused crowd, to take him off. Even then he managed to shout, 'Is it Grimsby they want? We'll give 'em Grimsby, won't we, boys?' which does not sound as if it means much but earned a roar of approval from other fellow-townsmen.

So right from the outset the game was played in the wrong kind of atmosphere, less like cricket than a football match — as if this was Sunderland playing Newcastle United. You can't really blame the players for all that happened.

Everything went well for the first few overs. Brandon was settling back into a semi-doze, instructing me to wake him if anyone looked like being out or anything exciting. And then Alan Keeler, one of our opening pair, was manifestly out LBW. It was so patent that Alan himself was already taking his first sullen steps pavilionwards when a shout from the boundary told him he hadn't been signalled out. By a happy coincidence it chanced to be up to the Riddleford Umpire to decide.

'Wow — is that within your unwritten limit?' Brandon laughed.

Jim didn't laugh. 'Harry's gone too far this time, you mark my words. He's let it go to his head, like. We'll pay for this later, I tell you.'

After the groans and boos had subsided, play continued. But now there seemed — or was I just imagining it? — a new grimness on the Grimwick faces, in the expectancy of the fielders, in the bowlers' new aggressiveness. Their fast bowler, Billy Robson, who had so distinguished himself in Riddleford on Grimsby's birthday, was sending them down almost faster than light. At the other end their spin merchant was doing things to the ball that looked like trick photography.

By the end of the first hour's play nerves were frayed, tempers were on the edge of breakdown. The weather didn't help — that close oppressive low cloud which is so powerfully claustrophobic. The usual phrase is that the atmosphere was electric, and I can't think of a better.

Through this atmosphere the fast bowler sent down a sudden crafty one. The batsman, a stolid unimaginative type, nicked it uncomfortably straight towards second slip, level with the ground, seemingly scraping the tips of the grassblades. Slip hurled himself at it, sprawled on the field, clutched with his hand, and caught it just off — or was it just *on*? — the ground.

Thunderous cheers greeted the feat. Half the crowd stood up. A few groans came from narrow-minded partisans, but most were ready to applaud the brilliant fielding. . . .

But once again the umpire whose decision it was happened to be the Riddleford man. There was a breathless hush right out of the copybook. And then he shook his head to the appeal. Not out.

This time all hell broke loose. The fact that there was quite an element of honest doubt made no difference. Jim shook his head. 'Harry shouldn't of done it. I said we'd pay for it, didn't I, now?'

The Grimwick team gathered round their captain and looked furiously at the Riddleford batsmen who stood silent and embarrassed at their creases. In the centre of the field all was tremulous and quiet, the white figures motionless against the dark grey sky and the unnaturally bright green of the grass.

Round the boundary on the other hand confusion was supreme. Not far from us a couple of hefty types were solidly bashing at each other, grunting, without a word, egged on by their neighbours. From all quarters yells of abuse and obscenity were hurtling towards the Riddleford Umpire, who stood stockstill out in the field like a snowman. The Riddleford Captain started walking out from the pav, though what he had in mind to do goodness knows. A bottle (Riddleford Brown Ale, I noticed) soared towards him and bounced only a few feet from him. He walked on regardless.

At the centre of the field the Grimwick Umpire was advancing menacingly on his colleague. The two batsmen had joined company and were standing together, clutching their bats as though they thought they might at any moment have to defend themselves to the death.

Some inquisitive members of the crowd were starting to encroach on the field, and the police were having an uneasy time trying to quieten things down. Jim just stood there shaking his head. 'He didn't ought, Harry should of known better. He shouldn't of done it. . . .'

We looked out over the heads of the spectators. Fighting seemed to be spreading, and though the weather seemed to damp down the sound, we were vaguely aware of a menacing seething in the crowd. The Grimwick Umpire was just coming up to the Riddleford Umpire who awaited him with folded arms . . . the Riddleford Captain was just coming up to the Grimwick team, who awaited him like a beleaguering army receiving an emissary from the besieged city . . . anything could happen.

And then, out of a sky which nobody had had time to notice because there were so many other things to catch the attention, dropped divine intervention. The low sagging clouds ripped apart and, in the nick of time, Rain Stopped Play.

XLIV

I WENT down to see Dennis at Seth's a few days later because Joe Higgs had given me the tip-off.

Seth's Sanitary Drainpipe Company is the nearest thing to industry you'll find in Riddleford. No cooling towers soar into the heavens, no skyscratching chimneys blacken the sky for miles around: tucked away in the hem of Riddleford's outskirts, you'd hardly know Seth's was there if you didn't know it was there, if you see what I mean.

Most of the men who work there live just round the corner. Their work is bang on their doorstep, so even if

Seth lacks some of the advantages of a big modern factory, you don't get some of the drawbacks either. True, there's no Works Canteen, no Welfare Officer, no Sports Club. But there's The Compasses next door, the fields slope down to the factory fence, and home is just down the street.

And there's none of the impersonality of the big works. Say you want to complain to the Management — what d'you do? You look around for Seth. He'll be somewhere about, stomping down the yard in his battered boots or even working at your elbow to load a delayed truck, more like a furnaceman than a bloated capitalist.

Everyone works hard at Seth's, but it's in the spirit of a family working into the small hours tarting the house up for Christmas. The place looks like Jarrow-in-the-Depression but really it's disgustingly prosperous. There's a big demand for drainpipes, what with all these new-fangled houses having baths and toilets and all, and the hill behind Seth's seems to be solid clay. So every dawn great truckloads of clinking pipes go clattering down the High Street and away along the main road to the wide world.

I walked through the Main Shed, full of serried ranks of half-baked drainpipes, up the rickety wooden steps and into the upstairs loft, the long wooden gallery where Dennis was working.

For Dennis is a skilled worker. He does the moulded jobs and comes to work in a suit and shoes and wears white overalls at his bench. Moulded jobs are special and hand-made. Anyone can make drainpipes pure and simple — the kind you see stacked on building sites or by roads with ROAD UP signs. But Dennis produces sophisticated pipes —

right-angle bends, complex joints, and, when called for, those wonderful deep-glazed ornamental urns beloved of Municipal parks, with floral reliefs, to be filled with nasturtiums or dandelions and shattered in the course of time by the stones of nasty small boys.

In fact, how I first met Dennis was when he had moulded some extra-special bowls to stand in front of Lady Jane's Cottage, donated by the Friends of Grimsby, and I had to write the affair up for the *Courant*. Often enough since then he's been a useful contact — a foot in another world, the world of those who never get quoted or praised or even noticed at all by the *Courant*, except when Top People deign to extend a patronising hand.

Dennis was working on a double joint as I came up to him, patting the soft clay with care so that you would hardly have guessed it was soft as plasticine. He looked up and grinned as I leant my back against the bench beside him, but went on stroking his joint. I offered him a cigarette: he wiped his hands down his overalls and took one.

'Thanks, Geoff boy. . . . How's the world with you? Written any good newspapers lately?'

'Oh, not so bad, y'know. How's it treating you?'

'Can't complain, you know, Geoff boy.'

There was a brief silence while we puffed our cigarettes. Then, the ritual observances done with, I went on. 'Been talking to Joe Higgs.'

'Oh yes? Haven't seen him in — oh, must be weeks.'

'He was telling me he was talking to Jack Dodds last night. And how Jack was saying you'd told him about some meeting your wife said your brother-in-law went to, over

Grimwick way. Some professor there, Joe said Jack said you said there was.'

'That's right. Yes, Alice said Arthur was most impressed, she said. Of course he thinks a lot of hisself — I mean Arthur does. You don't want to credit a word he says three-quarters of the time. But he came home full of what this professor johnny had been saying about how it wouldn't be any time at all before all the tourists were going to Grimwick instead of here.'

'You don't know anything else he said, do you?'

'Well, no, you know. You see, Alice doesn't really care much for politics. She didn't say much at all really.'

'Could be a nasty business, couldn't it?' I suggested.

'What could?'

'A nasty business for Riddleford, I mean.' I was curious to know what Dennis, as a member of the other world, thought of the Grimsby Affair. 'If all the tourists started going there instead of here.'

'Good riddance to the bleeders, I'd say.'

'Well, okay, but think of the money they bring.'

'I suppose that'd make a difference. . . . I don't know, though. Would it?'

'You ask Joe Higgs, next time you're by. Ask him how he'd like to manage without their trade. Ask anyone who keeps a shop in the town.'

Dennis nodded thoughtfully. 'Hm, I suppose so.'

There didn't seem to be much else I could extract from him — it seemed to have been something of a wild-goose chase. I turned to leave. 'Well, if your sister remembers anything more, or finds out something, you might tell me, will you?'

'I'll do that, Geoff boy.'

'Oh, and if she could tell us this professor's name . . .'

Dennis frowned. 'Why, you know, Geoff boy, I fancy she did mention that, now you remind me. Queer sort of name it was too, not one that you'd forget. Only I seem to have gone and forgotten it, all the same, sod it!' He patted a fresh lump of clay with his hands as though that might help him to remember: and perhaps it did, because he suddenly looked up with the frown cleared off his face.

'I've got it, Geoff boy! I said it was a queer name. Nightie — that's what Alice said it was. Nightie, now isn't that a queer name for a chap to have?'

XLV

'HELL, we should have guessed!'

Brandon was furious with himself. He strode excitedly up and down the back parlour of The Fox & Chicks, where an emergency committee meeting was being held. 'Damn it, we should have seen it weeks and ages ago!'

Jane said she didn't see how we could have.

'We knew they had someone working for them,' Brandon said. 'All we had to do was put two and two together and add them up to Nightly!'

'Anyway, it's not awfully surprising,' she said. 'I mean, if

Dr Nightly's got a theory, it stands to reason he'll want to prove it.'

'If he was a true scholar,' Harold said, 'he wouldn't be *trying* to prove his case. He'd be sitting back in Oxford waiting for it to prove itself.'

'If he's up here in person,' said Hilda Bunting grimly, 'I'd like to know what he's up to!'

'We don't know any more than that he's giving lectures,' I said. 'There's nothing unethical about that, is there? He's got this theory, as we all know: it's only natural he should want to persuade people that he's right. And Grimwick is one place where he's sure to get a good reception — it seems a rational place to start looking for converts. I dare say he's read about the things that've been happening, and that's why he's come up here. Just because more vulgar-minded people are hoping to cash in on his theories doesn't mean we have to hold *him* to account.'

'But there's more to it than that,' Brandon burst in. 'Don't forget that leaflet that Miss Jobling and her chums got so steamed up about. We guessed then, didn't we, that some pretty learned character was involved? You've got to admit it looks now as if that character was Dr Nightly. In which case it seems fairly reasonable to deduce that he's probably been implicated right down the line.'

'Perhaps he came up here looking for new evidence,' suggested Jane. 'After all, evidence doesn't just find itself, does it?'

'*Faking* new evidence more likely,' put in Joe Higgs sardonically. He was as despondent as the rest of us. 'Know what, had a customer in this morning. Better make the best of it, Joe, he says to me, you won't have Grimsby's fans

184

coming in here much longer you won't! That's where things has got to — people saying that kind of talk right to your very face! Lucky for him there was the bar counter atween him and me, I don't mind telling you!'

On the table between our drinks lay scattered a heap of publicity material from Grimwick — all claiming Nicolas for theirs. Harold told us how he'd seen travel posters for Grimwick on railway stations with the slogan THE HEART OF THE GRIMSBY COUNTRY. Jane had read out an article from a French newspaper left behind by one of her customers, which had shown a view of Riddleford High Street and inquired CETTE VILLE — DOIT-ELLE MOURIR?

Mrs Bunting, too, had her share to contribute to the Committee's tale of woe. 'We went to see the Member this afternoon. He was worried, wasn't he, Harold?'

'Yes indeed,' Harold assented, giving what we took to be an imitation of Mr Egerton Smythe. 'We were worried. Worried — yes, and most gravely disturbed. This was indeed news of the — ah — most grave, should we say, most *disturbing* consequence. It behoved all right-thinking men to stand firmly in their posts, to fight and not to yield. . . . As for us, we would give the matter our most *earnest* consideration.'

Scrubby giggled, but not for long. The bitterness in her father's voice, and the general tone of the meeting, didn't lend themselves to anyone being cheerful, not even her. There was a long despondent silence. 'Drink up — plenty more where that came from!' encouraged Joe, but nobody seemed to want to drink, not even Hilda.

And then suddenly into the gloomy silence Scrubby spoke, carefully, as though she had been thinking about what she said for some time. 'You know, the person who's going to be saddest of all, if you ask me, is Mr Krankel.'

There was a pause.

Then Joe Higgs slapped his knee and said something undistinguishable.

'What's that, Joe?' asked Mrs B sharply. 'Speak up, can't you?'

Joe looked hurt. 'I said the kid's gone and done it.'

'Gone and done *what*? In heaven's name, Joe. . . .'

'Hit the nail on the head, that's what she's done!'

'What nail, Joe? Be sensible, for goodness' sake!' The little room had suddenly taken on an extraordinary air of tension.

'Mr Krankel — the American, you know, the one who started Geoff's Foundation, and gave all that money, and . . .'

'Yes, I know, Joe — of course we all know who Mr Krankel is.' Mrs B, like the rest of us, was more than slightly on edge. 'What I don't see is what he's doing in this discussion. Of course he'll be sorry. So will we all. Do we have to run through the list of all the people who are going to weep when Riddleford hands Nicolas over to Grimwick?'

Joe waved his hands impatiently. 'Oh, you don't see what the child is after! She's the only clever one amongst the lot of us, the rest of us are so blind we just didn't see!'

'See what?'

Harold put his spoke in. 'I think I know what our daughter means.'

'Then please be good enough to explain it to me — quickly,' said his wife. 'I seem to be the only thick-headed person present. Kindly elucidate in words of one short syllable, as suitable to the mentally retarded.'

Harold calmly continued. 'What Sabrina means isn't just that our distinguished benefactor will be sorry about the loss. She means to imply that we might make use of this sorrow, isn't that so, Scrubby? Mr Krankel is a potential ally. A man of his — well, to put it bluntly, his means, might even take steps to prevent the loss ever happening. After all, Mr Krankel is a man of both wealth and influence: we could use both of those to help Nicolas.'

Mrs Bunting looked wide-eyed at her daughter, who had sat still all these last few moments like a serene oriental teacher while his disciples debate his exegesis. 'You really said all this?' she asked incredulously.

'Well, mummy, I just thought . . .'

'Sabrina Bunting, I see you are your mother's daughter!' Hilda was delighted now that she was no longer in the dark. She seized her offspring and enfolded her in a vast maternal hug.

Jane smiled at Scrubby over her mother's shoulder. 'So what do we do next?' she asked.

'Write to the man,' said Brandon, excited. 'Put him wise — and leave the rest to him.'

'But he reads the papers,' I said, 'he must know already.'

Brandon looked contemptuously at me. 'We can give him a bit more than the surface facts, can't we? We can give him the inside story. If he's really as keen on Nicolas as he pretends to be, that should make him sit up.'

Personally I didn't think it sounded particularly hopeful, but we all agreed it was worth trying. It was settled for some reason that I should be the one to write the letter. Joe called for drinks on the house, and we all drank Scrubby's health, including Scrubby.

A new hope had come our way at last. It might not be much of a hope, but anything was a change: what it did to our morale was nobody's business. Here was a chance which just might come off — a small chance that the New World might be called in to redress the helplessness of the Old.

XLVI

THROUGHOUT the Collected Works of Nicolas Grimsby there is but a single reference to the newly colonised New World — and that hardly a flattering one. In his *Second Satyr* he speaks of:

> *. . . the wilde American*
> *Who doth mid desarts huge and craggie rocks*
> *All hidious abyde.*

Poor Nicolas — how could he know how much his future fame was to be thanks to America, and largely thanks to one American in particular?

The Grimsby Foundation is but one instance of Omar Krankel's enthusiasm for Nicolas. Libraries across the width of the United States owe their extensive 'Grimsbiana' sections to him: it was he who subsidised the Modern Library edition of the Selected Works which, if it pruned out some of his finest poems, at any rate ensured that there were few homes throughout the United States which could not afford to have Nicolas at their firesides.

His too was the credit or the blame, depending on the way you look at these things, for the great revival of interest in Grimsbian problems. Throughout the world young men and women who otherwise would have had to go into trade or something equally disgusting have been awarded Krankel Fellowships to this university or that: and from the University Presses of Tokyo, Cambridge, Pisa, Mexico City or Melbourne there have poured forth the well-known *Krankel Studies in Grimsby*, monuments of misapplied research designed to be placed on the shelves of other universities and left to fust forgotten.

Again, Krankel Travel Grants have made it possible for coachload after coachload of American citizens, who have competed for the honour before the television cameras, to cross the Atlantic and visit every spot with which the name of Nicolas Grimsby has ever been associated.

What made Omar Krankel such an enthusiast for Nicolas?

Nobody knew, though there were legends aplenty. One story made him the descendant of a distant relative of Grimsby's, who had emigrated to America rather hurriedly in the eighteenth century immediately after the South Sea Bubble had burst, with a well-filled purse and a scared look over his shoulder.

Then there was another story which made him a Chicago mobster who had made a good thing out of selling out to Capone during the dry season, and who was now expiating his sins after Nicolas had appeared to him in a dream.

Perhaps nicest of all, there was the story that Mr Krankel

was a member of one of those quaint American religious bodies, the Latter-day This or That, who believe that if you search long enough among the poems of Grimsby you can find foretold the Survival of Hitler, the Height of the Pyramids, the First American Pope and the overthrow of all religious sects but their own.

When we wrote to him we had no idea what sort of man he was. We didn't know how old he was, what he looked like, anything at all about him. But we agreed that we couldn't lose anything by making the attempt.

Briefly I summarised the history of the Nightly theories and the Grimsby-for-Grimwick campaign. I explained that nothing official was being done, and why we amateurs felt compelled to take the matter into our own hands, but we didn't see what we could do.

From there on we left it to him. I signed it on behalf of all of us, marked the envelope PRIVATE AND CONFIDENTIAL in the top left, bunged it in the pillarbox, and we sat down to wait and hope.

'It'll take months to catch up with the old boy,' Brandon said pessimistically. 'With all that money, he could be anywhere — anchored off Bermuda in his yacht, holding barbecues with his Wall Street pals on his dude ranch in Arizona or fishing in Ontario from his personal seaplane. Writing like this to his New York office, we won't hear from him this side of Christmas — that is if he bothers to answer us at all.'

But Brandon was wrong.

XLVII

FOUR days later I was woken out of bed at the fantastic hour of three in the morning by the telephone. A call for me, said the girl's astonishingly wideawake voice, from someone I didn't hear in somewhere I couldn't catch, and would I take it?

The next voice was a man's voice, again perfectly wideawake and very smooth. Was this Mr Geoffrey Marston? it wanted to know. It was Mr. Krankel's secretary speaking — his *private* secretary — from Mr Krankel's country place — his *private* country place — in New Hampshire. Would I please hold the line?

Still in the dull stupor of sleep I sat huddled in the hall, clutching the phone, listening to the crackles. . . . They sounded as though, along the thousands of miles of cable tying me and New Hampshire together, there were mermaids and banshees who would have liked to horn in on our conversation, and were working off their frustration with a low pitter-patter murmur of just-out-of-earshot obscenities.

I couldn't think why Mr Krankel wanted to ring me at this godforsaken hour, and then I remembered that clocks are funny in America, they have Pacific Time and Atlantic Time and so on, and it was breakfast time now over there, and he would be having his orange juice and . . . or wait: just a moment: wasn't it supper time or more, and wouldn't the manservant be bringing him on a tray his late-night mug of Instant Postum?

I was desperately trying to calculate which when suddenly, taking me by surprise, a voice said 'Mr Marston?' — and there was I, talking right across an ocean at heaven knows how many dollars a minute to a millionaire I hadn't so much as been introduced to.

He told me he very much appreciated my very interesting but he guessed alarming letter. This Dr Nightly, now, was he the fellow who . . .? And Professor Bissentine, what did he . . .? And did the police . . .? And had the Mayor . . .? And the Public . . .? And the Press . . .? The questions rattled out fast one after the other, till I pictured Mr Krankel's brain as a giant electronic calculator, with my little facts being fed into it: and soon it would have all the facts it needed and the light would flash and the wheels would whirr and out would come the answer, pat.

And then abruptly he broke off and said he was going to drop everything, right then and there, more or less, and come over to Britain right away.

That shook me. I started to say something about how things really might not be so bad as all that and I wouldn't want to have him breaking off his engagements and all, only to find there wasn't really any need . . .

But Omar Krankel interrupted me. 'If it was important enough for you folks to write that letter, then it's important enough for me to come and see for myself.' He chuckled, and the chuckle came over rich and fruity even across the ocean between. 'Mr Marston, you may as well learn this here and now: so far as I personally am concerned, *anything* regarding Nicolas Grimsby is important to me!'

XLVIII

'Bᴜᴛ what did he *sound* like?'
    'He sounded like anyone else, darling. All Americans sound the same way when they're speaking right across the Atlantic.'

'How d'you know?'

'I'm just guessing.'

'Hm . . . but did he sound *nice?* Honestly, pet, you *are* inefficient! Talking with a real live millionaire and you can't even say what he sounded like!'

'But we'll know in a short while, when he arrives.'

'I want to know *now*. I don't suppose we'll get to see him when he does come, anyway. He'll spend his time in conferences with the bigwigs, and the most *we*'ll ever see of him will be his picture on the front page of the *Courant*.'

Each member of the Committee asked the same questions and I was soon tired of giving a thrust-by-thrust account of my dead-of-night conversation.

We kept what we had done very much to ourselves, especially after I had received a highly exciting letter from Mr Krankel's secretary saying that Mr Krankel planned to visit Riddleford incognito, keeping his presence quiet until he had sized up the situation for himself. So we would oblige him by not informing the Press or any other authority. And would we also make arrangements for his reception as soon as he let us know when he'd be arriving: though he gave no hint of when that would be.

From then on we were all on tenterhooks. For two days I
kept getting phone calls where mysterious voices like in spy
thrillers would mutter cryptically 'Any news?' in muffled
tones as though The Law were hot on their tracks. At the
Courant offices I found it hard to explain away the sudden
access of popularity, so I invented a crisis at the Foundation:
when there were calls for me at the Foundation I would
irritably exclaim 'Oh, not Grasmere *again*!' and put on the
martyred expression of a harassed newspaperman. As I
walked past The Clay & Wattle one lunchtime out rushed
Jane on to the pavement, still with a handful of cutlery in
her hand. 'Has anything happened yet, pet?' she shrieked to
the surprise of passing tourists.

'Darling, if it had I'd have told you,' I said, but she didn't
believe me. Every one of the Committee thought me perfectly capable of holding out on them. The third day wore
through and still no message came. Whenever I was at
home I thought someone might be trying to contact me at
the office or the Foundation; whenever I was away from
home I pictured the phone in Mafeking Gardens ringing,
ringing, ringing into vacancy. . . .

And then at last, on the third night, the Post Office phoned
a cable through to me. It was quite simple—

ARRIVE HEXHAM AIRPORT ABOUT
TEN PM THURSDAY KETCHUP

'What's it mean, "Ketchup"?' Jane asked.
'Alias. The letter said he wanted to be incognito. I sup-
pose that's the name he's chosen to be.'
The word was passed round. Rooms were booked at The

Grimsby Head for Mr Ketchup: and we wriggled on our tenterhooks till Thursday arrived.

XLIX

'HE might be early, you never know,' said Mrs B, so it was nearer nine than ten on Thursday night when we huddled into the waiting room at Hexham airport.

Hexham airport isn't one of those grand places with control towers and radar and fog lights and news theatres. Just a windsock and a stretch of concrete and corrugated-iron hangars where ageing mechanics with droopy moustaches could be imagined at work with primitive hand-drills on fabric-covered biplanes held together with wires. We sat in the converted nissen hut which served as waiting room.

'Well, Sabrina,' Harold Bunting said to his daughter, 'don't forget that this was all your idea in the first place. So if he's furious at us wasting his time dragging him over here, we'll blame it all on you — right?'

'Oh pooh!' she said.

'I must say I don't honestly see what he's going to do even when he's got here,' Jane said. 'After all, he doesn't live here like we do, he doesn't understand what's going on. If *we* can't do anything, I don't see why he should think *he* can!'

'Nonsense, child!' said Mrs Bunting. 'Mr Krankel is an American, and all the world knows Americans can do simply *anything*!' Brandon looked very smug and tried to look as American as he could. 'It stands to reason,' she went on, 'if you've enough push and enough money and are quite unhampered by any manners at all, you *must* be able to do anything!' Brandon stopped trying to look American and went outside to see if anything was happening. He came back and reported that nothing was.

We went on waiting and then an airport official came with an official-looking form torn off a pad. 'Message just through from your flight. Should touch down in approximately—' he consulted his watch, ' four and one quarter minutes.'

Scrubby dashed out, tugging Brandon by the hand. The rest of us clambered stiffly to our feet, stretched our cramped limbs, yawned, and walked out on to the airfield. It was still not entirely dark, though the first stars were to be seen dotted across the underwater-coloured sky. The distant hills were black where the sun had just set. We stood in a group, not going too far from each other, each gazing up into the sky where any moment now, like a rabbit from a conjurer's hat, a piece of magic would happen and our saviour descend from the heavens.

A few minutes, and then we heard the first faint hum of motors, reminding of returning bombers in one of those tense British war films.

'Pity Joe couldn't have been here to see this,' Hilda said. 'We should have insisted he left the shop with Mrs Higgs and came along with us.'

Now a new light could be seen in the star-spattered sky.

A red one: then a green one: and then the machine itself, silhouetted against the sky, circling over the farthest sheds, then touching down on the grass and taxi-ing slowly towards us. A few figures rushed forward from the lighted sheds. Steps were placed against the sides of the machine whose airscrews turned over slowly catching the light as they turned. And then a door slid open in the silver hull.

Jane confessed afterwards that her first sight of Omar Krankel had not impressed her as much as she wanted to be impressed. I think we all shared some of that disappointment.

Our hero looked, frankly, like any other American tourist. Later, when we got to know him, we could have kicked ourselves for thinking any such thing. Perhaps the same goes, though, for all American tourists: perhaps none of them is the mass-produced imbecile that his exterior suggests? Perhaps they are like Chinese — you have to get to know them before you realise they're not the same one over and over again, like stage armies in Shakespeare who run off one side, dash round behind the backcloth and turn up again, panting, where they started.

Followed by his secretary, Mr Krankel walked towards us. He was short and pale, and had on a plain grey suit and plain grey tie with a plain gold pin in it and a plain grey hat. He looked about fifty, only as with most Americans you couldn't tell for sure: they're as old as they feel and Mr Krankel didn't look as if he felt very old. You could have lost him in the crowd on any Riddleford pavement: a typical American businessman on a typical American vacation — the pathetically comic one, the one you know humiliating things are going to happen to the moment he appears on your cinema screen.

He introduced himself to us. 'You must be the one I spoke to on the telephone,' he said to me, shaking me happily by the hand. 'Learn to speak up, boy, learn to speak up!' He beamed at each of us: as he shook hands with Brandon, 'Glad to find at any rate one fellow-country-man in the party!' he said.

In no time he had had his passport examined and his cases customed, everything going much smoother and faster than any time *I*'ve arrived in England, so I should think his efficient-looking secretary — now presented to us by the name Clifford — must have said something to somebody somewhere. It was only a matter of five or six minutes before everyone at the airport was satisfied that it could be no great danger to England if Mr Krankel were set loose among us.

Half an hour later Mr Ketchup had duly registered at The Grimsby Head. Over a late supper — once again Clifford must have performed a miracle, Riddleford hotels like hotels elsewhere in Britain not being accustomed to putting themselves out for their guests — the millionaire started to cross-examine us. While the efficient secretary hovered silently round us, filling our glasses and lighting our cigarettes, we told our new friend all he wanted to know.

The masterly way in which his mind sorted out the situation, pierced right through to the fundamental issues, gave me some idea of the qualities which had made him the great tycoon that he was. Yet for all his ruthlessness, I felt we were treated not as subordinates or stockholders but as partners in an enterprise — fellow-members of the board at the very least. It was clear that he didn't feel what I had feared he might feel — that we had brought him here on a wild goose chase — by the great concern he showed at everything we told him.

He wanted to know everything. . . All about us, first, who we were. Then all about Riddleford and all that had happened since he was last in England. Then Dr Nightly, and the various incidents that had followed the publication of his book. And, finally, *why* we were doing this: why, when nobody else was doing anything to save Nicolas, we were sticking our necks out?

That was the hardest question of the lot, but we managed to find words for the answer, or perhaps Omar Krankel guessed what we could not say. At the end of it all, he knew as much as any of us. 'Looks as if I did right to drop over like this,' he said, wiping his mouth with his napkin and lolling back in his chair. 'Seems as though our Nicolas has got himself in a jam.'

Clifford poured him a generous scotch and soda. 'Well,' he continued, 'we don't want to let it get us down. In fact what I suggest here and now is let us get ourselves a good night's sleep. Then in the morning we can mull over a few basic thoughts. How does that suit you, eh?'

L

BRANDON and I went round to The Grimsby Head next morning, skipping what might very well have turned out to be a fascinating seminar at the Foundation on the significance of the colophon in pirated editions of seventeenth-century drama.

Mr Ketchup, so they told us at the hotel from amid the horse brasses and warming pans in the vestibule, was certainly up and about. Indeed they believed he was in the garden.

He was. We went through to where the sun was beating down on a gardener and Mr Krankel, deep in conversation. The sound of our footsteps made him turn towards us. 'Aha, there you are. I'm just picking up a few tips about my borders. Funny thing, I can manage most things, but borders I've always tripped on. Now I know why. Roughage — that's what they need. Like bowels. I've been starving my borders of roughage all these years.'

On a striped garden swing-seat a book lay open — Lemuel Nightly's book. 'Catching up on my homework,' Mr Krankel explained. 'I generally get to read everything they write about Nicolas, but there's such a heap of it these days, it takes a man all his time to keep abreast of just the reviews. This must be one of the ones I passed up.'

He riffled through Dr Nightly's pages, then threw the book down. 'The way I see it, this Nightly hasn't any too much to go on. It's convincing all right, if you accept his basic platform. But who's going to do that unless they're out of their mind? Or unless they see some gain in it for themselves?'

He asked what we thought. We agreed — it was a fine logical structure, but to get from the ground floor any higher you had to make a little mental jump: the staircase didn't stretch the whole way. If you didn't mind making that one little jump, you could manage the rest without a qualm of giddiness. Mr Krankel nodded.

If he had formulated any plan of action, it didn't show for the moment. 'Know what I'd like to do this morning? I'd like to have a look round the old place. It's quite a few years since I was last in Riddleford — we need to get re-acquainted.'

So the three of us wandered about the town all morning. We visited The Birthplace and I pointed out the modifications to the Statue: we stood in the queue at Lady Jane's Cottage and I pointed out Dennis's urns. We stuck our noses into Meg's and overheard old Sid Grimsby rating the Warden because nobody had come to repair the valve in his television set. 'Don't tell me that old faker's still breathing!' Mr Krankel marvelled. 'Grumbling must keep one young — I should try it sometime!'

Finally we dropped into The Clay & Wattle for a cup of coffee. The tea-shop was new since his last visit, and he was delighted beyond measure: he couldn't stop congratulating Bill and Shelagh on their décor. There was a little misunderstanding when Jane came across to take our order — he got to his feet to offer her a seat. I explained as best I could that she *worked* here, and after a momentary embarrassment he declared he was enchanted. 'Weren't any such charming waitresses last time, not that I can remember,' he smiled.

After our coffee we walked on down to the riverside, where we sat in deck chairs at 3d. each in the bright September sunshine. The first hearty tourists of the day were setting out two by two in punts and skiffs on the reedy Riddle, seeking discreetly weeping willows behind whose underhanging fronds they could settle to a spot of serious snogging.

For a while we sat and watched the sunlight on the water, saying nothing. Then Brandon, sensing that our companion might be in expansive mood, asked, 'How come you ever got so caught up with Nicolas, Mr Krankel?'

There was a pause while the millionaire continued to gaze out across the river. I wondered if Brandon had gone too far. But no, Mr Krankel turned back towards us and asked, 'Why, does it seem so funny to you?'

We hastily protested that no, it certainly didn't. 'It's just that, well . . .' Brandon began.

Mr Krankel laughed and waved away his protestation. 'Well, it certainly seems funny to me, I can tell you that! To think that your Foundation wouldn't exist, that neither of you would probably be here at this moment, if it wasn't for the magical power of bathroom fittings!'

LI

MR KRANKEL laughed again. 'Bathroom fittings!' he repeated. Burrowing in his pocket he fished out a packet of cheroots. 'Here, draw on one of these while I tell you about bathroom fittings.'

We lit up. The rich cigar smoke shimmered in the sunshine. The slop of water and distant squeals from the boaters came over at us.

'There's no secret about it — that's how I started. Lavatory basins and literature, that's how it's been with me. For years, though, more years than I care to remember, it was lavatory basins alone — *bigger* lavatory basins, *better* lavatory basins, *more* lavatory basins!

'I was lucky, of course — there's no country in the world so sold on keeping clean as the States. John Q Citizen was washing to my profit as well as his — and in the end, though neither of us knew it then, to Nicolas Grimsby's. I think Nicolas would have liked to think that it was *he* who gained whenever a Washington stenographer stepped into her shower or a Texas oilman scrubbed the grease off his hands.'

Mr Krankel chuckled. 'Maybe business seems to you fellows a dull affair? Well, I don't see myself as any knight in shining armour, tilting my lance against the WashWise WaterWare Company of Sykesburg, Mich., as some up-holders of the Great American Dream would probably wish me to see myself. But I've enjoyed myself, I will say, and only a fool would fail to be grateful for that.

'And you know as well as I do, if you enjoy a thing, chances are you'll succeed in it. My company moved onwards and upwards, and the higher the faster, till after a while it got so I didn't have to push any more. All there was for me to do was sign a few documents, look sly at board meetings and kindly at staff fraternisations, and that was all there was to making a fortune.

'By now, you understand, I'd gotten to be a fairly wealthy fellow. It was a bad year when I didn't have my picture in *Fortune* a couple of times, spouting my opinion on booms and recessions. Sometimes I had my secretary cook up some spiel: to everything else I maintained the role of Financial Wizard by saying cryptically No Comment. They'd never have believed me if I had told them the truth— that in those days I didn't know the first thing about anything at all outside of bathroom fittings.

'What brought this home to me was the crazy folk who wrote to me suggesting ways I could spend any millions I had to spare. Playwrights seeking an angel who'd stage their three-hour poetic dramas on Broadway. Scientists wanting to launch their projectiles across the Pole or the Pacific or up at the moon — anywhere, it didn't matter, so they got launched some place. Fellows who knew just where Long John Silver stashed his loot, fellows who could lay their hands on the Lost Continent of Mu or the Lost City of Atlantis if I'd just stake them to a pick and shovel and a few hundred grand. And any number who were concerned about the eternal welfare of my soul, ready to cure all my spiritual troubles — for of course I have spiritual

troubles the way I have duodenal ulcers: they're an occupa-
tional disease. I had the chance to buy myself a stake in
any number of private heavens — I could end my worries
by morally re-arming myself — I could purchase a First-
Class ticket on the Celestial Railroad for the price of a
steady subscription to the Fifteenth Church of the Divine
Revelation of Mount Jellyhokum.'

Omar Krankel smiled. 'And then one morning there was
this letter from your Birthplace Trust, here in Riddleford.
Seemed the birthplace of Nicolas Grimsby was about
to collapse any minute all for want of a few hundred
dollars.

'Now, I've always liked Grimsby's poetry, more than
most people's. I know there's a lot of it is thought a bit on
the raw side — but that was a different age, I tell people. I
always liked the swashbuckling get-up-and-go of those
early verses — yes, and the calmer reflective ones, later on.
Fact is, whatever mood you're in, Nicolas has a poem to
match it. And another thing, he never tastes like a man
who's been three centuries in his grave. He could be your
next-door neighbour, and you know you'd hit it off with
him if he was.

'So I slipped over here — anonymous — to peek round for
myself. It was just about this time of year — the end of a real
English summer. Riddleford looked pretty nice. . . . Well,
I gave them what they needed for The Birthplace, and a
bit over for one or two little tidying-up jobs. And after
that, I don't know myself how it came about, I grew more
and more involved in Grimsby and Riddleford. From then
till now, you could say, Nicolas Grimsby has been my
biggest hobby horse. . . .'

Suddenly he broke off and looked at his watch. 'Say, isn't Mrs Bunting expecting us for luncheon? Time we were moving, isn't it?'

On our way to Deep Thatch we called for a quick drink at The Fox & Chicks: Mr Krankel was introduced to Joe Higgs who — after carefully drying his hands on his apron — shook hands heartily with the American.

'What'll it be, sir?'

'It'll have to be a quick one, Mr Higgs.'

'A drop of scotch, maybe?' The landlord poured out the largest scotch I have ever seen, and waved aside the very idea of payment.

Mr Krankel drank his drink appreciatively, then said we really must be going but he hoped they'd meet again soon. Joe said he hoped so too as he ushered us to the door.

When he saw Deep Thatch he was quite delighted. 'I've seen the house on earlier visits,' he told Mrs B, 'but I'd no idea such charming people lived in it!'

'He's a champion handler of compliments,' commented Brandon. 'I wonder does he plan to recapture Nicolas by blinding the enemy with a barrage of flattery?'

LII

LUNCH was over. Throughout the meal Mr Krankel had kept the conversation to generalities: now he solemnly put down his coffee cup on the lawn where all the Committee were sitting, and said, 'Before we do anything else, I think I owe it to you folk to explain my position here, and the way I see this business so far.'

He beamed round at us. Nobody said anything but Sabrina coughed. 'This business isn't my business strictly,' he went on. 'I don't know any of the folks here, I don't have any ties here. All I've done is donate a little money to the town, and that's not a very spiritual relationship, is it?

'And even if my money did entitle me to a small say, this isn't a case for a businessman. It calls for scholarly folk, and by no stretch of the imagination could you call me that, not even now that I'm a Hon. D.Litt. of Carlisle University. My only excuse is this, that all the people who should be acting in this crisis don't seem to be lifting a finger — except you folk and, let's face it, there aren't many of you, are there?

'From the look of things, now is the time for all who love Grimsby to come running to his assistance. This isn't an affair where common-sense and reason count for much. If Grimwick thinks it can pull a fast one over the rest of the world, well, we have to fight back with the same weapons. We've got to take steps.

'What steps, you ask, don't you? Well, I have one or two

little ideas I'm playing with at the back of my head: but if you don't mind I'll keep them to myself just for the present. I'm not very sure about them, you see. In fact' — he pulled himself out of his deck chair and on to his feet — 'in fact I better start on them right now, if you'll excuse me. No time like the present, they say.' He bowed to Mrs Bunting. 'Thank you for a most delicious luncheon,' he said, and waving farewell to the rest of us he simply took himself off.

We looked at one another in astonishment. 'Well!' said Hilda Bunting, and though she said nothing more it was plain she wasn't too impressed by the way our new saviour was going about his business. For myself, I thought of that over-large scotch Joe Higgs had given him, of the sherry that Mrs Bunting had forced on him before lunch and the wine she'd served with it and the brandy she'd produced afterwards. . . . Whatever could he be up to? I wondered.

LIII

IT was not till late the same evening that I learnt what Mr Krankel had been up to: and then I learnt with a bang.

He sent word by Clifford — would I come along to his hotel, he asked, despite the late hour? Of course I dashed round to The Grimsby Head as fast as I could pedal, and leant my rusty black bike with sneaking delight among the Daimlers and Lagondas.

I found Omar Krankel sitting in his room looking placid and comfortable, as though he had been sitting there all day long. He offered me a drink and I had a drink. He offered me something to eat and I happily nibbled some smoked salmon sandwiches — not that I'm particularly fond of smoked salmon, but it was a chance to taste how the Other Half eats.

'I'm willing to wager you people must have been a little alarmed when I took myself off this afternoon — am I wrong?'

'Well . . .'

Mr Krankel laughed. 'I was afraid so. But the why of it is this: I didn't want to tell you what I had in mind to do because you might have tried to stop me. Now, though, I have to take someone into my confidence, and I thought I'd try it out on you first. Okay?'

I felt a slight tingle of alarm up my backbone. What had he in mind? Not — please God — something criminal, an assault on Mayor Duncible or an attack on the new portrait with dynamite!

'I won't ask you to guess where I've been. I'll tell you instead. I went to call on Dr Nightly.'

He laughed at my dismayed astonishment. 'It seemed the obvious first move.' Obvious? I wondered. Yes, it was obvious. Just as putting your head in the lion's mouth is the obvious way to find out if he bites. I said as much.

Mr Krankel nodded. 'But if it's the only way? Someone had to stick their neck out, and I figured it might as well be me.'

I asked how he had found Dr Nightly. 'The porter at their Town Hall in Grimwick, he directed me.'

I gave up. Either everything suddenly became easy when this man came near, or there was something inside him which made him take instinctively the quickest way every time. How long would it have taken *me* to find Dr Nightly's lodgings, I wondered — and me supposed to be a journalist: what subtle questions I should have felt it necessary to ask before I learnt what I wanted! Perhaps, I conjectured, Omar Krankel had got where he was by merely always doing the obvious . . .

'He was mad when I barged in, real mad. He'd have kicked me out straightaway only he's not the kicking kind, and I think the surprise of hearing my name and seeing me there in person caught him on the wrong foot. And perhaps I didn't look as though I'd let myself be kicked out either.

'Men like Nightly are tough customers to handle, Geoff. They're not really sane, you see. Trouble was, I didn't latch on soon enough. I should have seen from the first he's one of those folk whose ideas are four-square in their heads, stuck there for keeps. Only a clever job of undercutting can set them loose enough to knock away. Did you ever try getting a limpet off a rock? It's the same treatment: a sudden surprise is the only way.

'But, as I say, I didn't latch on soon enough, and when I did his alarm bell was buzzing. He's a clever fellow, no doubt about that. I called on his better feelings. That was a fool thing to do, and I knew it, but it didn't stop me trying — though I knew men like Nightly don't have better feelings, they get dried out early in the game. You can't touch their hearts any more than the limpet's: too many layers of shell. Nightly had his soft underside hidden away from me and he meant to keep it that way.

'I tried everything in the book. Asked him to think of the people of Riddleford: he answered that for his money Riddleford could jump in the Riddle and drift out to sea. . . . Well, we had a bit of a showdown, flinging words and being none too dainty about it. Then in comes this other character, this Town Clerk, name of Pike. Walter Pike.

'As soon as I clapped eyes on him I knew who we were up against. Here's the man who set the ball rolling, I said to myself. Smooth as silk he was to start with, but he soon saw that soft soap wasn't getting him anywhere with me. So he switched to calling names. "Scared about your interests in Riddleford?" he asked. And then he turned on Nightly. "Tell him how you've proved it all!" he shouted. "Show him the evidence!" But Nightly just smiled in his watery way. "What, show *him*?" "Why the hell not?" asked Pike. And Nightly said for him not to be childish.

'I couldn't make out what was going on — I looked from one face to the other in vain — then all of a sudden I got the idea. "I think I see it all now," I told them, and I said to Nightly straight out he was selling his scholarship short and I was on to his dirty deal.

'Brother, was he mad!' Mr Krankel smiled at the memory. ' "How dare you, sir," he shouted, "how dare you!" just like a play, and he went on repeating how did I dare, how did I dare, as if he were stuck like an old phonograph.

'Then Pike stepped forward and said I must stop slandering one of the world's leading scholars, and he wasn't going to stand by while Nightly's name was smeared by a — let me get this right — a bloody foreigner who just because he's got money thinks he's God Almighty, and why didn't I keep my nose in my own washbasins and out of matters

I knew nothing about? How d'you like that?' Mr Krankel laughed. 'Well, you know, I think even Pike realised he'd gone too far with that. He made a sort of shift with his body as if he could somehow grab the words back before they got to me.

'But, boy, he'd finally got my goat! Nobody's spoken to me that way in years! I think it does a man good to be in-sulted every once in a while — shakes him out of growing too complacent. But I wasn't standing for that, not on your life! "You don't leave me any choice," said I. "There's just one way to settle this, and that's the way it's going to be! Mr Pike, you will hear from my seconds in a very short while!" And, so help me, Geoff, that's the way it *is* going to be!

'Pike turned white as a sheet, and then he said, half choking, "Don't you worry, you old fool, I'll meet you!" — old, he called me, Geoff: *me, old!* And *he's* no spring chicken! "I'll meet you anywhere, any time you choose!" he said. So I said again he'd be hearing from me, and I stalked out of that office, leaving them both goggling after me like a pair of fish!'

LIV

I DARE say I was goggling myself. Had I heard him properly? Couldn't I have misunderstood? 'No, but listen, sir, you — you just *can't*!' I thought I sounded pretty feeble, even to myself.

212

'Why not? I don't have to have those kind of remarks made to me!'

'But a duel! It's fantastic,' I protested. 'It's illegal, they won't let you. . . .'

'There are a good many things we men don't permit each other to do,' said Mr Krankel slowly, 'and quite right too. I'm *for* the Law. But every now and then a problem comes along that a handy tool like the Law isn't big enough to shift: that's when you need a bulldozer.' He patted his stomach with a smile. 'Temporarily I'm being a bulldozer.'

'But violence doesn't solve anything,' I objected.

Mr Krankel laughed. 'Oh, I'm with you there, you bet. That's exactly what I'm going to prove to them. These gentlemen think they can win their point by violence — they've used violent means all along. Well, Geoff, I'm calling their bluff. I'm going to force them to more violence than they ever contemplated. And directed at them personally, what's more — not just the community as a whole.'

I didn't say anything to that. What could I say?

So there I was, with another tumblerful of much-needed drink in my hand, still unbelieving but unable to disbelieve, discussing the arrangements for a duel with a bathroom-ware millionaire.

LV

THE reactions of the Committee were varied. Hilda Bunting literally wailed. 'I *said* he wasn't going to be much use to us, but this is *worse*, this is a positive *spanner in the works*! What in heaven's name does he want to push some personal quarrel into the foreground for — we've got quite enough on our hands already. What's this man Pike got to do with it anyway?' It was quite characteristic of Hilda to confuse the duel's immediate pretext with Mr Krankel's ultimate aim, but in the shock of first hearing the news the mistake was forgiveable.

Her husband saw a little more clearly what the American was at. Harold's imagination was caught by the gallant gesture, in which he saw a revival of the ancient custom of settling a difference by single combat. 'But at the same time, Geoff, this *is* the twentieth century. . . .' He would have tried to talk Mr Krankel out of it, but I told him it would be no use: the millionaire's mind was made up, and nothing could shake him out of it.

Jane had never actually *seen* Walter Pike but she conjured up a picture of Grimwick's over-zealous Town Clerk that made him sound like a villain from a Victorian melodrama, capable of cutting Mr Krankel into tiny little bits or spitting his head on a pikestaff outside Grimwick Town Hall. 'Can't somebody stop him?' she moaned, and she too had to be convinced that no, nobody could.

Scrubby, I need hardly say, was thrilled to the marrow. With the X-ray eyes of childhood she saw through Omar Krankel's externals to the Galahad beneath. He was her podgy but verray parfit gentil knight, who would return from slaying the caitiff Pike with his head a trifle bloody, perhaps, but certainly unbowed.

Joe Higgs was deeply respectful. Ever since licensing laws were first thought of, publicans have had to be the most law-respecting of citizens, and it is hard to shake off the mental habits of a lifetime. But in this instance Joe could see that a higher law was involved. Omar Krankel's right to defend his honour against all the Pikes of this world transcended fears of local bench or county assizes.

'So the Grimwick authorities and Nightly are in this together,' Brandon exclaimed, 'and it's Mr Town Clerk Pike we have to hold responsible! He's been there all the time, behind all that's happened. . . .' He had only one word for Mr Krankel's action: 'sporting'. His fellow-countryman really was doing the decent thing. Ivanhoe couldn't have been decenter, nor Hotspur nor Lancelot nor David Copperfield himself. 'I'm sorry, though, because to tell you the honest truth I don't think he stands a dog's chance. . . .'

LVI

You only need to have a unicorn in your garden a day or two before you discover it isn't half so fabulous as people make out. The incredible duel became more and more believable the longer we lived with it.

It amazed me that Walter Pike had accepted the challenge. But it didn't amaze Harold Bunting, who explained it by saying, 'It's the Northumbrian in him. Up in this part of the world they still believe in all manner of things they've forgotten or left behind down south — honour and things like that. I can't say I know this man Pike, but I wager Omar Krankel has pricked his honour on a sensitive patch!'

So on both sides of the fence everyone connected with the duel came to regard it as — well, no, not an everyday occurrence exactly, but as something that *might* have occurred every day even if it hadn't.

Mr Krankel insisted on appointing me his official second. I didn't want to one bit, but I could hardly refuse. Besides, it was something of a privilege. Walter Pike's choice was blatantly a snook cocked at Riddleford — Fothergill Jones, formerly the Official Guide of our town. After being dismissed by Riddleford Council he had, not surprisingly, run off to Grimwick. Pike's selection was a nicely calculated insult, and one which gave us a hint what mood the Grimwick Town Clerk must be in.

'Cor,' Mr Jones told me when we met to decide on procedure, his lizard's eyes flashing, 'Mr Pike isn't half feeling

stroppy. Real mad. Says he's going to have your chap's
blood if it's the last thing he does. . . . You should hear him
go on: not much between him and the nuthouse if you ask
me.'

There did not seem to be any strong chain of affection
binding Mr Jones to his employer. 'I'll tell you the truth of
it, Mr. Marston,' he confided, leaning nearer with a smell of
carbolic soap. 'I don't know that I care much one way or the
other, you might say. 'Course it wouldn't hardly behove me
to speak anything actually ill of Mr Pike, would it, after all
he is my employer, but I believe I am not transgressing the
limits of loyalty when I observe that if he dropped dead
at this instant I wouldn't be the first to rush forward with
my half-crown for the wreath.'

'But you think he's in the right?'

'How d'you mean, "right", exactly?'

'About Nicolas Grimsby. I mean, you yourself — well,
you . . .' I felt embarrassed, but I needn't have — Fothergill
Jones had no more sense of shame than he had of right or
wrong.

'Oho, you mean about me leaving Riddleford? Well,
the fact of *that* matter was I couldn't very well refuse. I've
got a conscience and all, same as the next man. But when a
man comes after you with *that* kind of an offer, well, *you*
wouldn't have turned it down. Nobody could. . . . Double
your salary, just for telling the visitors different. . . . Well,
what do the visitors care what you tell 'em? Sheep, that's
what they are, bloody ignorant sheep. They listen to me
because they've paid to, and I talk to them because I'm paid
to, and that believe me is the long and the short of the matter,
Mr Marston. Mind, I could have told Mr Pike it wasn't

doing any good. But I said to myself, well, if he's got all this lolly to chuck around, I might as well grab what I can, see? So I did.'

I saw his point, and tactfully switched the conversation to the business before us. With the help of the Public Library we managed to agree on the form and procedure to be followed. As challenged party, Mr Pike had the choice of weapons. Pistols, Mr Jones said Mr Pike wanted. Then there was the question of distance. And number of shots. And the referee. And the doctor. And all sorts of technicalities about commands and seconds and times. It took us some hours of cogitation, with constant reference to Chekhov and *The Three Musketeers*, but in the end we got it all settled.

LVII

IT was through Fothergill Jones that we learnt how Nightly and the Grimwick faction had become involved together in the first place. Whether the facts really were as Fothergill represented them I don't know to this day, but they are plausible enough.

More than anyone else, Walter Pike, the Town Clerk, was the driving force behind the Grimsby-for-Grimwick campaign. All his dreams, all his energies had — from the moment he became a municipal employee — been devoted to a better, more prosperous Grimwick. And a very praiseworthy frame of mind, too.

But then he began to be haunted by this fatal dream, that Nicolas Grimsby could be proved a son of Grimwick. Where the idea came from, Fothergill couldn't tell me: one can only surmise that Pike's mind had been touched by some echo of the Shakespeare/Bacon dispute or that he had heard of the cities of Greece contending for the honour of having given birth to Homer. Or maybe, reading through old county histories, he had come across those early suggestions that Nicolas was no native of Riddleford?

But whatever its origin, it was in pursuit of this dream that he visited Oxford and paid a call on Dr Nightly. What, he asked the scholar, did the academic world think of the theories that Nicolas was not born in Riddleford? Dr Nightly told him then and there that with so little to go on no scholar could take the theories seriously. If there were more *evidence* now . . .

Walter Pike went back to Grimwick alone, but he carried with him Dr Nightly's words. And a few months later Nightly received a letter from Grimwick informing him that new evidence had, indeed, been unearthed, and the Grimwick Council would be honoured if Dr Nightly would care to come and examine it.

Was Dr Nightly suspicious? We don't know. But up he went to Grimwick in any case, to take a look for himself. For if the evidence were in fact conclusive, this might well be the making of his career.

He was quickly disillusioned. A first glance from his scholarly eye showed him that the new material was worthless. He said so — and Pike put his cards on the table.

Well, so there *was* no evidence. But if Dr Nightly would like to manufacture his own, Grimwick would be happy to supply him with whatever assistance he needed. And it was added that a large, a lavish, financial reward went with the job.

Twenty thousand pounds was the sum named — and that is a large sum for a poor scholar with a meagre fellowship and nothing put by. Who could blame Nightly for being tempted?

He was tempted — and fell. To keep the records straight, he was appointed Municipal Archivist, though no public mention of the appointment was ever made. Under this concealment he prepared the dubious evidence for his *New Evaluation* and helped to fake the 'second portrait' for its postscript.

Fothergill's story left many things still unexplained, but it went a good way to account for all that had happened. Clear, now, was the combination of scholarship with a well-planned, well-financed campaign.

And Walter Pike's own actions were clearer now. Scheming, scoundrelly, evil — we had thought our enemy all these: but now the picture presented to us was one of worthy ambition over-reaching itself, of single-minded partisanship determined to attain its ends by whatever means lay to hand.

And if we were no less determined to fight till the last to prevent Walter Pike fetching our Nicolas away, we had a little more respect for our enemy now that we knew more about the motives that were spurring him on.

As Jane said, 'It doesn't make what they're doing any better, but it makes it easier to understand.'

'The French say that to understand all is to forgive all,' I remarked.

'Oh, they do, do they? I don't know that I'll go *that* far. But perhaps I don't hate him quite as much as I did. . . .'

LVIII

'I WISH today were over and done with,' said Jane, as she brought our after-lunch coffee to the table. 'I've already dropped one bowl of sugar and served a corned-beef salad to a vegetarian. Bill and Shelagh must think we've quarrelled.'

'I suppose we're "also serving",' I suggested gloomily.

'Whatever we're doing, I don't like it,' Jane said. 'I mean — well, just think of it: that poor man may be cold and *dead* this time tomorrow, and all for nothing.'

'Don't be so sure it's all for nothing.'

'Well, if that's the only thing that'll shake up the people of Riddleford, then they don't deserve to be shaken. They just bloody well aren't worth it!' She swept together a heap of dirty crocks and carried them out to the kitchen, leaving me sitting with nothing to do but drink my coffee and brood on the unbelievable event.

Unbelievable: yet here it was, laid on to take place within the next twenty-four hours, the fuse already lit and no prospect of anything interfering. As Jane said, this time

tomorrow *anything* could have happened — it was so
fantastic that it was hard to face up to at all. Somewhere
inside me I felt that people don't do such things, that they
are confined to army officers in Chekhov and Dumas. It
was so absurd that I couldn't get my emotions to grips with
it at all.

At the Foundation, earlier in the afternoon, it had been
hard for Brandon and me to keep our gloom and anxiety to
ourselves amid the trivial gaiety of the other students. I
asked Brandon did he want to come along with me to The
Clay & Wattle? He said he was off to the movies. I asked
what was on and he said he didn't know. He was going
regardless, to sit through all four houses, slap in the centre of
the front row, and if that didn't drug him into insensibility
nothing would.

I left the tea-shop and went home. Home was too quiet.
It was the middle of the afternoon, and all up and down
Mafeking Gardens I could hear domestic noises happening.
I tried to drown my thoughts with jazz: and just as I'd got
nicely settled, through the rich soprano sax of Bechet the
telephone came slashing.

It was Hilda Bunting. 'Geoff dear, is that you? . . . My
dear, isn't there *anything* we can do? Isn't it our *duty* to
inform the police — aren't we compounding a felony? . . .
Stool-pigeons? No, of course I don't want to let him
down . . . well, if that's really what you think . . . but I
shan't sleep a wink the whole blessed night . . . I'll go to bed
with Ian Fleming and perhaps he'll take my mind off it
all . . .'

I went out for a walk: it didn't do anything to help. I
looked at the happy sightseers gambolling beside the Riddle,

and I wanted to rush among them like a prophet and stop them enjoying themselves.

As early as it could possibly be her knocking-off time I went to collect Jane from The Clay & Wattle. Rather than make ourselves miserable in either of our own homes, we adjourned to The Fox & Chicks, only to find Joe Higgs not on speaking terms with the rest of the world. His mood spread throughout the house — the atmosphere of gloom in the Public Bar sat heavily and uncomfortably on the shoulders of the drinkers, ignorant of its cause, and many a regular left earlier that night than usual.

A visiting salesman tried to arouse Joe's interest in the topic of paramount importance at the time to everyone in the county except ourselves — the vexed question whether or not 'Slosher' M'Gee had been strictly out for the count in the heavyweight semis at Carlisle — a question on which every right-thinking man in the district had a quite un-shakeable opinion one way or the other. But tonight Joe was not to be drawn. With a brief remark he killed the discussion dead.

The salesman raised his eyebrows eloquently at the rest of us, muttered how some people didn't seem to be quite their usual selves, did they, not tonight they didn't; and left to see if he had any better luck at The Feathers.

So Jane and I sat on one side of the bar and Joe leant dismally on the other, and we did our best to drown our sorrows in drink. And as usually happens the alcohol in our drinks seemed to have evaporated completely. At closing time we were all as sober as new-born judges, and we walked home in a state of utter and complete misery.

'I wonder how Mr Krankel's feeling,' Jane reflected.

'He was cheerful as you like earlier in the day,' I answered. 'When I saw him he didn't seem concerned in the slightest. I asked did he want me to come round tonight, and he said quite happily no, thank me all the same. He didn't even think he'd need me tomorrow morning: Clifford would drive him down and he'd meet me there, it would be less suspicious, he said.'

'Sounds as if he's happier about it than we are,' Jane said, as we paused outside her house.

'Could well be.' I said I'd call for her about five in the morning. We kissed goodnight solemnly and I walked miserably back to Mafeking Gardens.

LIX

SEEKING a discreet site for the encounter, Fothergill Jones and I had determined on a secluded clearing in the pines at the far end of a shrubberied lane named Potter's Path. It could be approached from two ends, which was rather convenient — one near the Riddleford Recreation Ground, the other out on the Grimwick Road. It was as peaceful and discreet as could be wished.

Tradition was with us. The peacefulness and discretion of Potter's Path have ensured that for centuries it has been used as the ideal location for any number of shady activities by the locals.

During the first few yards of the path the Riddleford Council, seeking for some way in which it can patriotically and at the same time cheaply say how pleased it is about Coronations, Military Triumphs, Royal Jubilees, Visits of Distinguished Persons, Deaths of Mayors and the Relief of Beleaguered Cities in distant corners of that far-flung Commonwealth of which, at such times, Riddleford likes to feel itself a part, has scattered seats at intervals. Here amorous Jacks whose Jills are not co-operating as well as they might, wretched Corydons whose Phyllises have gone off to the Regal with Damon, may pass their time in a useful manner by carving their initials — with, it may be, a tasteful heart-and-arrow motif into the bargain — in the municipal woodwork.

The farther from the town, the fewer and farther between the signs of life — the discarded cigarette packets and Crunchie-wrappers and hygienic rubber goods that have served their purpose. The seats grow sparser and the shrubberies thicker, and the natural vegetation becomes more and more suitable to clandestine goings-on.

What goes on on Saturday nights is nobody's business (except when Miss Jobling makes it hers). The evening air, dampened by the mist that rises after sunset from the limpid Riddle, is disturbed by guffaws and giggles and squeaks — 'No, Georgie, you mustn't!' — 'Oooh, that tickles, love: do it again!'

But nothing of that sort was to be heard this morning: the only sound was the song of the early birds and the swish of our feet through the dew-damp bracken. The grass beside the path was glistening and our shoes were black with wet: our breath came white and smoky in the dank October morning.

'Look — we're not the first,' Jane exclaimed. Looking down, I saw footprints in the dew. 'The doctor and the referee,' I suggested.

'The doctor?'

'Oh yes, there always has to be a doctor.' Jane asked who he was. 'From Grimwick — name of Blake. Officer of Health and all that, nice fellow. He wasn't frightfully keen, but said he owed it to himself to come — he's writing his memoirs, it seems, the way everyone is these days—*Fifty Years as a Medico in Darkest Northumbria*—said he wouldn't miss a chance like this for the world. Besides, Pike's his boss.'

'All the same, it seems a bit gruesome. . . . And what about the referee?'

'Hoylake Dunn — have you come across him? Rather a joke, I know, but he seemed the right man for the job. He's the Chaplain out at Gooseleigh — personal minister to the souls of the Gooses.'

'I didn't know they had any,' Jane said bitterly.

'I dare say they haven't. The story goes,' I told her, hoping to keep her mind off what we were about, 'old Otterburn asked the Provost of his College for a suitable chaplain — "Someone, you know, who'd do for Gooseleigh". The Provost had a pretty shrewd notion what his Lordship wanted. Young Hoylake only scraped a third, but he'd acquired a couple of blues. . . . At tea in the Provost's rooms Hoylake met Lord Otterburn and after two minutes of small-talk the conversation switched to the comparative merits of "over-and-unders" and "side-by-sides": and they spoke of nothing else but guns throughout the meal. At the end of which his Lordship whispered to the Provost that young Hoylake was just the man for the job.'

'I see why you thought him the right man for *this* job, too,' Jane said and shivered. 'It's all so bloody *macabre*!' I put my arm round her.

'I agree, Hoylake's a bit much. But he's one of the few people we could have chosen — who'd see that things go correctly. In fact he's almost too much of a stickler for doing it correctly, insisting on all sorts of bits of protocol which Jones and I would happily drop. Says if a thing's worth doing it's worth doing properly. . . . Perhaps it'll be some consolation to Mr Krankel to think that if he is killed it will be with all the right sorts of pomp and circumstance.'

'Oh don't!' cried Jane. 'Don't even *think* that he might be killed. I can't bear it.' We had both managed to forget for a while what a serious business this was that we were engaged on: now the remembrance came flooding into our minds again, and it hurt.

Neither of us spoke another word till we reached the point where Potter's Path emerges into the pine clearing.

LX

HOYLAKE DUNN was indeed already there, and Dr Blake also. Standing in a quiet huddled group under the pines were Hilda and Harold Bunting, Joe Higgs and Brandon.

It was just on ten minutes to six, my watch said. Everyone was solemnly introduced to everyone else, and then we stood in silence, waiting, as the first sun burst through the mist, slanting between the pines.

Suddenly Jane gripped my arm. I looked up and saw that — at the very same moment, one from the east and the other from the west — the two protagonists were approaching: Mr Pike accompanied by Fothergill Jones, Mr Krankel by Clifford.

Hoylake Dunn stepped forward and looked with raised eyebrows to me. I wondered had I forgotten some vital part of the ritual, and introduced him to Omar Krankel. 'You are fully conversant with the rules which have been agreed?' Hoylake asked.

Mr Krankel nodded. I looked closely at him: he seemed to have withdrawn into himself, but when he felt my look he glanced up and gave me a quick, abrupt wink.

Hoylake then walked across to where Mr Pike stood. There were more introductions — the faint hum of inaudible speech came to us through the air.

It was for most of us our first sight of our antagonist, and we all watched him with apprehensive curiosity. He looked less truculent, less Machiavellian than I had expected, but perhaps it was only that the present circumstances had subdued him. And there was still a certain swagger about him, even in the very way he stood and waited and glanced about him.

Now seeing for the first time the enemy we had talked about so long without knowing his identity, now finding him with us in flesh and blood, it struck me that it might be *his* blood, not Omar Krankel's, that would be spilt. That the tragedy might have this other face was something which had never occurred to us while the other possible victim was unknown.

On a portable table rested a heavy-looking leather case, from which Hoylake drew two gleaming pistols. 'His Lordship lent them to me,' he explained confidentially to Fothergill and myself as he unpacked them. 'Wonderful craftsmanship — made by Panucci of Verona in 1827. I tried them out in the Beech Walk last night — beautiful, really beautiful.' He took one in either hand and weighed them one against the other. 'Suit our purpose admirably.'

He was about to step forward with them when he checked himself and turned to me. 'I say, Marston, who gets first choice of weapons? Blow me if I remember!'

'Why,' Fothergill Jones said hastily, 'obviously the challenged party. My man, no doubt of that.'

I felt it up to me to stick up for my man, even though it didn't seem to matter in the slightest. 'You had the choice of *kind* of weapon. *We* select the actual firearm.'

Hoylake was perplexed. 'Toss for it,' Dr Blake suggested. Hoylake was shocked. 'Hardly in keeping with the dignity of the occasion, d'you think?'

'They toss at cricket, don't they? Even at Test Matches.'

'Why, so they do — must be in order. . . . Will you call, Mr Jones?'

Their pistols in their hands, the two duellists stood alone like ballet dancers waiting their cue. They had each shed their jackets. Mr Krankel's plain white nylon shirt billowed slightly above his trousers. Mr Pike's waistcoat stuck its points out sharply before him. Both stood stock still without a movement.

A gust of tiny breeze rattled the pine needles against each other. A cone fell lightly. Hoylake stepped forward into the centre of the clearing and called the two men to him. They approached warily.

'You will stand back to back. At my command you will each take nine paces forward and stand still. At my further command you will turn and fire. You will not reload and fire again until I give you a further command.'

A pause. Then Hoylake, standing back with Fothergill Jones and myself, gave the first command. The two men started walking — nine slow paces away from each other, no sound from the soft pine needles. The contrast between the short tubby American and the lean scraggy Englishman grew less marked as they separated.

The clearing was more hushed than ever . . . and that hush brought home to me what had got lost in the ritual of the preliminaries — the true nature of what was happening. There was a sudden panic, a rush of blood to my head that blackened my consciousness for a moment and lost the two white protagonists, the small huddled group of

230

spectators, in a mist. Then Hoylake said 'Fire!' taking everyone by surprise.

The two statues spun round. Simultaneously two shots crashed through the clearing, making so great a detonation that no sound could have been louder. Mrs Bunting shrieked: two puffs of smoke billowed round the two duellists.

When the smoke had cleared away and we returned to the senses which the shots had momentarily driven away — as they had sent all the birds for miles around flapping screaming out of their nests — everything looked as it had before. The two duellists were still standing like statues, facing each other, their pistols in their motionless hands.

'Christ, they both missed!' muttered Joe.

'How could they?' Hilda Bunting asked wildly.

'They did it on purpose,' Jane said.

'I shouldn't think so,' said Brandon, forcing, I could tell, a cool detachment over the excitement in his voice. He explained just how difficult it is to hit anything with a pistol — especially an unfamiliar one. He was the only person speaking: the rest of the group listened to him with half their attention, kept the other half on Hoylake. Clifford watched his master anxiously, twisting his hands in and out of each other.

Hoylake glared in Brandon's direction and became authoritative once more. 'Turn again,' he commanded. 'Seconds, take their firearms and reload. I shall give the order to fire as before.'

'Is this necessary?' asked Dr Blake, who looked white and shaken, as if he had enough for his memoirs.

Hoylake rounded on him, shocked. 'Of course it is.

There has been no injury, and they must fire again. It is a rule to which both have agreed.'

There seemed no answer to that. The guns were reloaded and all returned to as before, as in a stage rehearsal when the actors go back to the beginning again. The two men took their nine paces and stood again waiting. The tension returned. The sick feeling came again.

But this time Hoylake did not get the chance to give his command. There was the sound of trampling in the under-growth — so loud in the unnatural stillness of the morning that one might have fancied oneself in a jungle clearing, with some unknown game approaching. We heard indistinct shouting in the distance. And suddenly into the clearing burst an extraordinary apparition.

LXI

IT was dressed in pyjamas: maroon and yellow pyjamas, rather tasteless. And a violent orange dressing-gown, also rather vulgar. One foot was in a green bedroom slipper and the other was not. Black hair, long uncut, streamed in the air.

'Nightly!' hissed — and it really *was* hissed — Walter Pike, as the apparition halted in the middle of the clearing, panting frighteningly. It took the scholar a moment to gather his breath, but he said 'Stop!' in a hoarse cry as though we might ignore his intrusion and carry on as though nothing had happened. The two duellists had lowered their guns: like the rest of us they stood inactive, waiting for the intruder to explain himself. 'All,' he panted, tears in his eyes, 'all mistake. My (phew!) fault (whoof!) all time. Explain but (phew!) stop!'

But before Dr Nightly could make himself any more coherent there came more crashing in the undergrowth. This time it was a brace of policemen. They stopped dead when they saw us all, in obvious and not really surprising astonishment at finding so many of us in so out-of-the-way a spot at such a time of day. The two duellists hastily concealed their weapons behind their backs, and Walter Pike looked as though he were making every effort to efface himself.

The policeman caught sight of Dr Nightly. 'There he is!' one cried, and they grabbed the scholar by his collar. He twisted his turkey-like neck about but couldn't free himself. 'Right, now,' said the older and heavier policeman, 'you be quiet now.'

Their prisoner had recovered enough breath to say, 'What do you mean? Why should I be quiet? What do you think you are doing?'

Dr Blake stepped forward. At the unexpected sight of him the two policemen touched their helmets and looked taken aback. 'What is this all about, Sergeant Rumsey?' the doctor asked.

Well, the sergeant explained, the police station at Grimwick had received that morning a communication to the effect that at about seventeen minutes before six o'clock a strange person had been observed dashing down the main street in suspicious circumstances, let alone that the car in which he was dashing was considerably exceeding the statutory speed limit. The vehicle had headed for the Riddleford Road. The police, scenting something up (crime in Grimwick being monotonously confined to shop-lifting from Marks & Spencer's, affrays with bicycle chains on the common and now and then a sexual offence behind the bus station), had driven off in pursuit.

They came across the car run up on the grass verge at the Grimwick end of Potter's Path: the door was open as though its driver had abandoned it in a hurry, but there was no sign of an accident. They had set off in pursuit along the path: found a green slipper (which one of the pair still held in his hand): caught occasional glimpses of his gaudy clothes through the trees as they ran. And now they would be obliged if he would return with them to explain his conduct.

There was a pause as the sergeant finished his narrative, and every one of us stared at the wretched scholar. Dr Blake said, 'Let's hear, shall we, what Dr Nightly has to say to account for his actions here and now? I'll take the responsibility, sergeant. Perhaps something important has happened.'

The policemen let go of their charge reluctantly, and stayed near him to see he didn't try any funny stuff. Dr Nightly did not in fact look capable of trying any funny stuff: his long run had left him panting and coughing.

'Now, Dr Nightly . . .' Dr Blake said. There was a grim professional note in his voice as though he had caught the scholar pouring his castor-oil down the wash-basin.

'Oh, I was in a hurry, don't you see?' cried Dr Nightly. 'I didn't have time to change into anything else. You don't suppose I would have come out-of-doors arrayed in this manner if I had had any time to spare, do you?' The two policemen looked away at the sky and the trees, as though personally they would have believed anything of their prisoner.

'But *why* were you in such a hurry?'

'To be in time — what do you think?'

'In time for what?'

'Oh, don't be so *dense*!' Dr Nightly's voice broke into a shrill falsetto of impatience. 'In time to stop anything happening. Which thank heaven I was.' He looked round at Mr Pike and Mr Krankel as if checking them off present and correct.

'Now see here, Nightly . . .' Walter Pike said, stepping forward. But the scholar interrupted him. 'It was to prevent *you* I was in such a hurry, Pike.' His voice sounded melodramatic, but then we were all feeling melodramatic. 'Don't imagine I was concerned about *your* hide! But I was about *his*!' and he nodded towards Omar Krankel.

He drew his dressing-gown about him like a cloak and raised his tremulous voice. 'I've been making up my mind to this all the week. I had my doubts right from the start: now I have them no longer. I am here to tell the truth!'

'Nightly, you're being a fool!' But Walter Pike's tone of authority was wearing thin as though it had been nibbled at by doubts of his own, and the scholar ignored him.

LXII

GRAVELY the policeman handed Dr Nightly his second slipper. He slipped it on to his dew-wet foot, then straightened up and looked round at us uncertainly.

'You said you were here to tell us the truth,' Dr Blake reminded him.

'Yes. Yes, that's right . . .' The scholar seemed to gather himself up to speak. 'As I say, I've cherished doubts ever since this whole business began. But it was only when Omar Krankel came bursting into my office that I seriously began to ask myself, was I doing the wrong thing?

'Oh, of course you all will say I'd been doing the wrong thing from the start, selling my soul for cash.

'But will you believe me if I say there was *more* than just the cash? If any of you here have lived in the academic world, you at any rate may understand me. You may feel a touch of sympathy when I tell you what Walter Pike's deceitful suggestion meant to me. It meant a heaven-sent chance to pull a fast one over my fellow-scholars. A chance to show just how shallow and squalid are the artificial values of the academic world.

'I won't deny it, I enjoyed the work. What glorious fun it was making that second portrait, for instance — fun enough to forget the other, childish incidents, the painted statues and the silly picketing. And I've been kept so busy — busy lecturing, busy interviewing the Press, broadcasting, writing articles and letters — I simply haven't had the chance to turn in my tracks and look coldly at what I've been doing. . . .

'Until Omar Krankel appeared in my office the other day. It was when I saw him and Walter Pike face each other, it was then I knew the party was over. You see, they both — each in his own way — they both *cared*. To me it might be a game, but for them it was a passion. Pike had worked for this all his life — given Grimwick his loyalty, his respect and even his self-respect. To make Grimwick the home town of Nicolas Grimsby had become the overriding object of his life.

'But it didn't take me long to see that the American was in earnest too: and Walter saw it too. When the challenge came, Walter was ready . . . and of a sudden I found my little game wasn't funny any more. Between these two grand passions, my little flirtation was nothing: this sordid money-grubbing businessman has more real love for Grimsby than I have with all my learning and my scholarship! He is ready to risk his life for Grimsby: *I* would never have done that. And so I saw that I could not allow Grimsby to be taken away from this man. For Riddleford and its citizens I don't care a damn, but if there is justice anywhere, then Nicolas Grimsby belongs to Omar Krankel.'

Dr Nightly ended and stood silent, looking at the ground. Real life was beginning to seep back as the morning sunlight strengthened. There was only just enough of the theatrical atmosphere left for us not to be embarrassed by the scholar's last words, and by Mr Krankel when he stepped forward, still in his shirtsleeves, and took Dr Nightly's hand in his.

He tried to speak but couldn't. There were tears in his eyes, and behind him Mrs B was unashamedly dabbing

away with her hankie and clinging to Jane for dear
life.

For a moment the two men stood there, just looking at
each other. Then Joe Higgs exclaimed, 'Christ! Walter
Pike! He's scarpered!'

Yes, we saw as we looked around — Walter Pike was
gone. Nobody had seen him go, nobody ever saw him
again. He was gone, fled from Grimwick, fled from
Northumbria, fled from the sight of all that knew him,
vanished away in the bright autumn morning.

LXIII

Autumn inspired our Nicolas — his eye as ever on
the main chance — to point a characteristic moral:

> *As leaues in Autumn fall,*
> *So pretty Maydens shall you all.*
> *Your worth shall be forgot,*
> *As leaues to coal, so you to Earth shall rot.*
> *Yet when beneath the Dust*
> *You come to sleepe, as come you must,*
> *Ah, let it not be said*
> *As she was born, so did she die — a mayde!*

Autumn in Riddleford has always been, as Nicolas
thought it should be, a time for merry-making, even if —

outwardly at any rate — the merry-making doesn't take quite the form that Nicolas proposed to his lady friends. The summer season is the tourist season, when the people of Riddleford can hardly call their town their own. But by October the summer migrants have returned to their winter habitat to breed new visitors for next year: the worthy burghers are left to count their blessings and their bulging bank balances.

So now, before the town goes into hibernation for the winter: before the leaves fall in Mafeking Gardens and along Potter's Path and in the Beech Walk at Gooseleigh: before the snowploughs are called out on the Carlisle Road and the roads to the snowbound moorland villages are blocked by television cameras recording the gallant efforts of the authorities to rescue the starving villagers: now, before Nicolas Grimsby is wrapped in tissue paper and packed away till next season, Riddleford treats itself to a brief indian summer of private rejoicing.

October turned into November. And Riddleford's relief at the overthrow of the Grimwick conspiracy became mixed up with the celebrations of another plot that very nearly came off — Guy Fawkes Day.

Riddleford has always believed in doing Guy Fawkes proud. Well before October is out the kids are plundering back yards gathering winter fuel for bonfires. Shops that in the normal way sell anything from toffee to tintacks now add fireworks to their stock-in-trade. Exciting things that go WHOOOSH! in the night. Little peppery things to go SNAP! CRACKLE! POP! under Mrs Dodds from next door. Crimson Flame and Golden Rain. Wheels of Fire and Coiling Serpents and fire-breathing Javanese Dragons.

Bangs and flashes and every crackling twinkling sparkling device that the ingenuity of man has devised, from the soaring remarkable rocket to the Centrical Circumfuse Wheel.

This year everything was as usual, only more so. This year the town had the excuse to plan a Bumper Occasion, a Double Feature programme uniting the traditional festivities with this special attraction.

Most of the people of Riddleford had only the dimmest notion what it was that Omar Krankel had saved them from. They were aware that some danger had menaced them: but just *what* it was, how *big* it was, what *shape* it took, other than the traditional rivalry and envy of Grimwick for Riddleford, they didn't rightly know. No matter. Enough that from the heavens they had been sent a hero whose gallant exploits they could now proceed to celebrate. Any excuse for a beanfeast.

There had been no sensational Now-It-Can-Be-Told release of the Pike/Krankel story. Officially indeed no story existed. The police had been persuaded by Dr Blake that nothing criminal had happened. The two newspapers by mutual agreement had been magnificently vague, and only the flimsiest wisps of rumour had reached the national Press.

So it was a good two or three days before every child in Riddleford knew every detail of the facts . . . how Omar Krankel, snorting with fury, had swaggered into Grimwick Town Hall with a six-shooter in either hand, and had challenged Lemuel Nightly to come on out and settle it man to man. They knew how Walter Pike and his gang of hired desperadoes with curly black moustaches had basely sought to ambush the gallant American, and how the said gallant American had whipped out his guns and pumped lead into the dirty yellow-livered bastard till you could see daylight through him in seventeen places. . . .

Every boy in Riddleford knew it all, right down to the crimson blood dripping onto the pine-needles and Omar Krankel blowing the smoke off the barrels of his guns after the last shot had echoed through the woods and the carcase of the dastardly villain still twitched repulsively on the gore-soaked earth. Outside my cottage the kids had forgotten Davy Crockett and Dan Dare: a new folk-hero had been added to their mythology, and I dare say the ritual representation of his exploits will be part of the repertoire of Riddleford's youth for generations to come, widening and including the feats of other heroes as year succeeds to year. Round the corners of fences, through gaps in the hedgerow, as bike passes bike in the street, the guns will thunder, the white dust will rise beneath the drumbeat of galloping hooves: with a deprecating smile playing over his imperturbable features, Omar Krankel will ride forth to battle, toughest gunfighter that ever rode the Tombstone Trail, fastest man on the draw from Santa Fé to Grimwick. And year after year blood-chilling screams, convulsive shudders, will mark the last desperate moments of Walter Pike, "Toad-Eye" Pike, sneakinest hombre this side of the Riddle.

'Whooooooosh!' went another rocket, heading up towards a purple sky and giving up its ghost in a shower of hundreds and thousands.

'Tragi-comic, that's what I call it — tragi-comic,' Brandon declared.

I stopped watching the rockets and looked at him instead, huddling in his duffle-coat. 'What's tragi-comic?' I asked.

'All this.' He waved round at the students and faculty of the Grimsby Foundation, happily celebrating. 'The hideous spectacle of intellectuals letting their hair down. It's tragic because they can't do it. It's comic because they keep on trying.'

A few yards away Professor Bissentine was skipping wildly in delight — he had just carefully placed a thunder-flash under the bench where sat one of his colleagues. 'Look at that, for instance. Who would ever imagine that that man has discoursed to international conferences on the debt of Restoration Tragedy to Etienne Jodelle?'

'Don't you be such a blooming killjoy, Brandon!' shouted Jane above the crashing and crackling, hanging on to my arm and leaning past me to scream at him. 'Why can't you let *your* crewcut down just for once? At least Bubbles is enjoying himself, not like you, you old sourpuss!'

Bubbles certainly was enjoying himself. The thunderflash had been a huge success. In fact wherever you looked the Grimsby Foundation seemed to be having a perfectly splendid time. In the back garden — the dirty scrap of waste land generally described (by the British students) as 'the campus' — the materials for a colossal fire had been painstakingly collected over the past few weeks.

What with the duel, Brandon and I hadn't been able to put our hearts into getting ready for the Fifth. But now everything in the garden looked lovely —didn't it? Omar

Krankel was safe — wasn't he? — and Grimsby was safe and Riddleford was safe — weren't they? — and all was for the best in this best of all possible worlds, and we could let ourselves go — couldn't we?

For the past three days we had all been hard at work getting our Guy ready. All who had ever set eyes on Lemuel Nightly were called in as modelling advisers: and if after all our time and care the result wasn't much of a likeness, identification was assured by a large placard round his neck saying who he was supposed to be.

Now Dr Nightly was burning beautifully. 'Poor old fellow,' Jane said sadly as his second arm flared up. 'I think I feel rather sorry for him now that it's all over. I'm sure if I'd been him I'd have wanted to do just the same.'

Around the flaring fire the students were silhouetted, capering happily, leaping whenever an extra specially big bang banged, toasting sausages on the end of sticks in a hearty manner while they shielded their eyes from the glare, diving into cardboard crates for cans of beer which Omar Krankel had got Joe to send over from The Fox & Chicks.

So great was all this joy and jubilation that it was hard to remember that anything else was going on anywhere else in Riddleford. Only now and then if you looked up you were aware that other rockets than ours were cascading up there in the heavens: that bangs and pops besides ours were enlivening the night sky.

'. . . a new Art Form: one which combines the intrinsic stability of a constantly shifting light source with the concentric *one*-ness of the Catherine Wheel . . . plastic, and at the same time immutably affirming a universal theme. . . .'

It was Harold Caravaggio Bunting, once again launching

himself into uncharted seas of artistic experiment. And who was being the first to hear of it but Phoebe Stuart-Stotts, whose pudgy arm rested happily beneath his hand, whose wide eyes gazed at him enthralled. . . . How often in years to come would the girls of Jones College, Denver, hear how the famous painter had confided to her — in person and alone — his first tentative gropings towards the theory of Concentricism!

Catching sight of us, Harold strolled over with Phoebe clinging on determinedly. 'Well, Grimsby seems to be safe for Riddleford,' he said cheerily.

'Safe and sound,' I agreed. 'Riddleford can forget all about him till the next time.'

Harold looked up at me sharply. 'The next time?' He frowned. 'You sound a trifle bitter, Geoff.'

'I do?' I listened to the mental echo of my own voice. It *did* sound a little disenchanted, not quite tuned up to the pitch of the orchestra around me. 'I think perhaps that's because I *feel* a trifle bitter.'

'But *why*, pet?' Jane looked worried.

I tried to think why. 'All over the town they're dancing and singing, because somebody's come and done for them what they bloody well should have upped and done for themselves. And, you know, they aren't really grateful, not even now. They're only celebrating because they *like* celebrating. . . . Oh, if you ask them, they'll tell you they're celebrating because it's over: but *what*'s over they only dimly realise. They haven't learnt to recognise their danger — they won't know it any better next time. And next time, will they have a convenient deus ex machina to do their rescue work for them?'

I waved my arm to indicate the rejoicing throng about us. 'They aren't fit to have Nicolas; he's wasted on them, they oughtn't to be trusted with him. Harold, you say Grimsby's safe for Riddleford. Okay, but is Riddleford safe for Grimsby?'

Harold was silent for a moment. Then he said, 'Isn't it the same everywhere? Think of the other Riddlefords all over the world — Florence and Montmartre and Stratford and the rest. Is any of them any better? . . . Let's face it, Geoff, there's nowhere in the world really fit for him. *Inside* people — people like Omar Krankel — that's the only world fit for Grimsby.'

After a moment Harold took himself off, towing the happy Phoebe. He was right, I suppose. But I didn't want to have to face his facts. I felt bitterer than ever as I turned again to watch the carefree revellers.

'A most historic occasion, Mr Marston!' said a voice at my elbow: Bubbles in person. 'And in large measure, I am given to understand, one that we have you and your friends to thank for. Indeed, the entire Foundation owes you a debt of gratitude. . . .' He looked at Jane and me with a bright smile and ran off to play with his thunderflashes, over by the bonfire where Brandon was now pursuing Scrubby Bunting with a handful of squibs.

'A historic occasion?' Yes, and I thought how lavishly and lovingly the *Courant* would splash it across its pages. . . . Thank heaven it wasn't me that would have to write the story. Young Alec had been assigned to it — he was at it now, dashing about Riddleford on his Vespa, gathering facts and figures . . . noting the busy crowds in The Fox & Chicks, where the part that Joe Higgs had played was doing his

trade a power of good . . . observing Sam Hartpool and
Miss Jobling miraculously dancing together round the
bonfire in Market Square . . . taking down in his impeccable
shorthand old Sid Grimsby's comments ('Best ruddy Guy
Fawkeses I ever saw!') . . . the Reverend Dwindle skilfully
touching off a giant rocket and sending it skimming past
the spire of Saint Bridget's to burst over the Primitive
Baptist Chapel in a blaze of stars. Alec would be charting
the triumphant progress of Omar Krankel through the
town — greeted everywhere by citizens who might not be
clear what he had done but were delighted that he'd done
it — borne down the High Street on the shoulders of the
crowd and set down outside The Clay & Wattle to make a
speech which they cheered like crazy . . . all this young Alec
would be noting down, mustering his reserves of cliché to
describe this historic occasion in the historic language it
deserved.

I was glad someone else was writing that article. I didn't
want it to be me who grovelled for hackneyed phrases
which would flip slickly out of Roget's *Thesaurus* and on to
the pages. What Omar Krankel was and what he had done
was something there aren't the words for now that the Age
of Chivalry is dead: better keep quiet altogether than trot
out the usual patronising blarney — Our Deliverer, Our
Champion, our any bloody thing at all.

I didn't want to prate of our fast-rooted traditions, our
cultural heirlooms, of torches handed from hand to hand
which we must keep burning in trust for those who come
after. . . .

I didn't want, above all, to write about the people of
Riddleford — these simple country folk living their simple

country lives in this simple country town as their forebears have done across the annals of our rough island story — I didn't want to ladle out the syrupy sentiments and I was glad I didn't have to.

I grabbed Jane's hand and moved towards the group prancing round what was left of Dr Nightly. That was what I wanted. I needed to be bounced from one crest of enjoyment to another, jolting every thought and memory out of my head, so I could forget the whole damn shooting-match.